Wild Boys

–Logan–

EVERYTHING'S NAUGHTIER AFTER DARK...

Billionaires After Dark Series

Melissa Foster

M&F

ISBN-13: 978-1-941480-13-7
ISBN-10: 1941480136

Cover Design: Elizabeth Mackey
Cover Photography: Wander Aguiar

WORLD LITERARY PRESS
PRINTED IN THE UNITED STATES OF AMERICA

A Note to Readers

My fans have been asking for a darker, sexier version of the Bradens, and I'm proud to bring you the Billionaires After Dark, written in the same raw, emotional voice as the Bradens and my other romance series, with naughtier language and amped up heat levels. These smoking-hot billionaires move fast, love passionately, and fall hard. If this is your first Melissa Foster novel, you have a whole series of loyal, sexy, and wickedly naughty heroes and sexy, sassy heroines to catch up on in my Love in Bloom romance collection (Snow Sisters, the Bradens, the Remingtons, Seaside Summers, and the Ryders). The characters from each series make appearances in other Love in Bloom books. There is a complete book list in the back of this novel.

Be sure to sign up for my newsletter so you never miss a release!
www.melissafoster.com/newsletter

Melissa Foster

Chapter One

BACHELOR PARTIES WERE the worst. Stella Krane couldn't understand why guys needed a wedding in order to go to a bar, drink their asses off, flirt with strangers, and talk about it for the rest of their lives. *Remember when...?* It was like a rite of passage for uptight businessmen. *Real* men took it to a hotel room, hired strippers, and fucked the hell out of them in ways their pretty little wives wouldn't ever let them. She cringed at the thought. She wouldn't want a man who did that. God, what was going on with her?

There was a time when Stella had dreamed of being someone's pretty little wife, but that was before Carl Kutcher. Her gut twisted with the realization that he was getting out of jail in four days. The man had stolen every dream she'd ever had—and who knew when he'd steal her life. She no longer held on to the fantasy of a doting husband, a few kids, and a white picket fence. Now she was just happy to be alive.

"Hey, sweetheart, how about a little sugar with my drink?" drunken asshole number six asked as he leaned over the bar. He was with the bachelor party and had been drinking for the past few hours. Five guys with wedding rings pawing, groping, leering, making lewd comments, and trying their best to live out a stilted fantasy.

Stella eyed his wedding ring. Damn, she needed to get off

1

tonight—and she wasn't thinking about getting off work. It'd been too many months since she'd gotten laid, and she'd had it up to here watching everyone else play out their dirty fantasies. She longed for the feel of a man's hands on her ass while his cock drove hard and deep inside her, allowing her brain to escape reality for a while. Stella wasn't *really* a one-night-fuck type of girl—but right then, boy did she wish she were. She missed the feel of a hard chest pressing against her and the deep, naughty whispers of a man telling her how much he wanted her. She'd never been that down-and-dirty girl until Kutcher. He'd sparked a side of her that she hadn't known existed, a dangerous, rebellious side that turned her on in ways she never imagined possible. But that was before things went bad and Kutcher showed his true colors. *The bastard.* She refused to even think of him as *Carl* anymore. Now he was just *Kutcher.* Kutcher had taught her many things, like that men pretty much suck. They lie, cheat, and sometimes…they beat the hell out of you.

She narrowed her catlike green eyes at the mildly attractive, dark-haired sure thing before her and practically purred, "How about I get you another drink and you go home and fuck your wife's sugar-coated pussy?"

Jaw slack—check. Eyes wide—check. Oh, look, a bonus. Mr. I Want Some Sugar backed away from the bar.

Some days she felt like a babysitter and a whore at once, but hey, working at a bar in New York City might not be like running her own interior design business in Mystic, Connecticut, but it kept her alive. She missed Mystic. She missed the harbor, the safety of the small town, her friends. She missed her mother most of all. Her mother was battling cancer, but like everything else in her life, she'd had to sever all ties with her mother in order to keep her safe from Kutcher.

Stella had lived in Mystic her whole life. Until Kutcher. *Fucking Kutcher.* Slick-tongued, hard-bodied, and unfortunately, hard-fisted Kutcher. She'd dated him for only a few months before he showed his true colors. His possessiveness knew no boundaries, and she'd barely escaped with her life. No, this might not be Mystic, and she might have had to leave everything she knew and loved behind, but at least she'd survived—even if she had to spend the rest of her life pretending to be someone she wasn't.

She felt the eyes of the man at the end of the bar on her again. He wasn't part of the bachelor party—at least that was a plus. He'd come in an hour ago, ordered a Jack and Coke, and hadn't moved anything but his piercing blue eyes—which had tracked her every move—since. He wore an expensive suit coat over a white dress shirt open at the neck, exposing a swath of sexy chest hair. Perfect for running her fingers through when she straddled him.

Lord.

What had Kutcher done to her? How had she gone from being a proper Wesleyan girl to a slutty-minded runaway? She'd met Carl Kutcher at a party for one of her interior design clients. He was tall and dark with a trim beard, eyes as black as night, and a quiet confidence that gave him an aura of importance. Stella had learned too late that there were two sides to the man who seemed too good to be true. He moved like the sea, calm and alluring one minute, angry and dark the next. His moods changed with the wind, and when they did, he left no room for escape.

Stella pushed thoughts of Kutcher away and tried to concentrate as she served up two more drinks, feeling the heat of

Mr. Blue Eyes rolling over her breasts as she leaned down to wipe the bar. Hell if it didn't make her entire body go hot. She'd been through enough over the past few months and knew better than to let a man intimidate her, but every time she tried to meet his gaze, she couldn't do it. He *was* intimidating, in an edgy sort of way. Everything about him, from his thick dark hair and chiseled features to his iridescent baby blues, screamed sex, power, and intensity. Even his scent was musky and sensual, like liquid amber. She'd like to roll around in his scent, revel in the feel of his big hands on her breasts, her rib cage—

What the hell am I thinking?

She was pretty sure that her landlord, Mrs. Fairly, wouldn't be thrilled with a midnight romp in her basement bedroom. Stella wasn't exactly the quietest of lovers. She'd been lucky enough to find a place to stay where she could pay cash for rent and didn't have to provide her social security number for the lease. She had to be completely untraceable, which meant no credit cards, no checks, and never using her ATM card. Fucking Kutcher had tracked her down everywhere she went, which was why she'd finally left Mystic and come to the Big Apple to disappear.

So far so good.

A large hand landed on the bar just beneath her chest, fingers splayed. No wedding ring, soft, unmarred hands, manicured fingernails. The hand of a wealthy man, that much was for sure. Her eyes traveled up to a thick, masculine wrist, suit jacket stretched tight across flexed biceps, to the piercing blue eyes she'd been fantasizing about. Her breath caught in her throat at the intensity of his stare. He circled her wrist with his index finger and thumb, drawing her eyes downward and sending her heart into panic mode. She'd been here before, restrained by Kutcher, unable to break free.

She forced her mind to function and pulled her arm free, rubbing it as if it had been burned.

"Sorry, darlin'. I didn't mean to frighten you." His deep voice slithered over her skin as his gaze softened, penetrating in a different way. Not intense and threatening, but the kind of heated gaze that felt safe and seductive at once.

Stella swallowed her initial fear, gathering her wits about her. She wasn't a meek girl. At five foot five, a hundred and twenty-five pounds, she was curvy and solid, and until Kutcher, she'd had the confidence to match her strong body. Now it took a few minutes to reclaim that confidence. She hated that even after a few months Kutcher's memory could still swamp her.

"Just one of those nights." With her words his eyes went from seductive to assessing, his dark brows knitted together, and he lifted his hand from the bar and rubbed the sexy scruff peppering his chin. A slight smile curved his full lips as he glanced over his shoulder at the loud bachelor party, then turned and lowered his voice.

"Yes, I can see it is." He held up his glass. "When you have time?"

"Sure." She picked up on a faint Midwestern twang that came and went and pictured him in tight jeans, cowboy boots, and a Stetson. She turned to mix his drink, thinking about the man behind her whose eyes burned a path through her back. She wondered what he did for a living, dressed like that and alone at a bar on a Friday night. A man with eyes like Chris Pine's, a face like Channing Tatum's, and a voice like melted chocolate, which made her want to lick him from head to toe. Unaccompanied on a Friday night? *Gay?* No way. Not with the way he'd been eye-fucking her all night. *Freak?* Probably.

On that lovely thought, she turned and pushed his drink across the bar. "That'll be—"

He placed his hand over hers, stopping her cold and making her body hum and rattle with fear in equal measure.

"I know how much it is, darlin'. Thank you."

She withdrew her hand from beneath his, instantly missing the connection. It'd been too damn long. She just might have to break out her battery-operated boyfriend tonight and satisfy the itch she'd been ignoring since arriving in the city.

He handed her a twenty. "Keep the change. You're new here." He sipped his drink, eyes locked on her.

She worked the register, trying not to think about the man behind the generous tip. *Yeah, right.* She wiped the bar to give her hands something to do besides wanting to touch his again, and eyed him warily.

"I started a few weeks ago."

"That explains it. I've been in and out of town the last few weeks. Where'd you work before this?"

She leaned one hand on the bar, finding her confidence once again. It came and went like the wind these days, and she was glad when it decided to blow back in. The guy's eyes turned sultry, and a rush of excitement heated her insides. It'd also been a long time since she'd been *properly* flirted with.

"Around," she answered, toying with him.

A blond guy leaned in over Midwestern hottie's shoulder. "Can I get another gin and tonic, please?"

She took his glass and turned away to mix the cocktail.

"She's so fucking hot," the tall blond said. Stella hoped to hell he wasn't talking about her. She'd heard enough about her ass, her tits, and her fuckable mouth for one night.

She handed him his glass and he shoved a ten across the bar

with a wink. A fifty-cent tip. *Jesus Christ.* She used to earn six figures, and now she was schlepping drinks in a bar for peanuts.

The familiar mantra played in her head like a broken record, giving her strength and perspective.

At least I'm alive.

I'm alive. I'm alive. I'm alive.

LOGAN WILD COULD watch the sassy bartender all night long. He was a regular at NightCaps, his buddy Dylan's bar and his go-to place after a long week of tracking down cheating spouses, embezzlers, and thieves. He hadn't been interested in getting laid when he'd come into the bar. Two busty blondes had satisfied that urge earlier in the week when he'd been in Memphis working on a case, but now he was reconsidering his evening plans. There was something about the sharp-tongued brunette with plump lips he'd like to see wrapped around his thick cock and eyes that said "fuck me" and "don't touch me" all at once.

She moved at record speed as the night wore on, dodging offers of sexual escapades with married men like bullets and always with a smart-ass retort. But she wasn't hardened, not like most of the sharp-witted women around New York City. She held her head high, like she wouldn't take shit from anyone. But as soon as those big talkers turned their backs, he swore he saw her exhale and her body become less rigid, more feminine. Not that she wasn't feminine when she was talking smack. With a body meant for loving, a mouth made for kissing, and hands that gripped a glass with surety, she was a fine mix of strength and delicacy.

He didn't know why he was assessing her so intimately. Usually Logan was a one-hit wonder kind of guy. Meet 'em, bang 'em, leave 'em behind. The pattern worked well for him over the past thirty-two years, and he was in no hurry to change it. He'd seen too many guys fall into marriage only to hire men like him a few years later to catch their wives with the gardener or the UPS guy. Monogamy was for the birds, and he didn't fucking care to tweet.

One of the drunken douche bags from the bachelor party was at her again. He'd heard her shut him down earlier, but the guy had had plenty more to drink, and he was leaning across the bar, reaching for her.

She stepped back, lowered her adorably pointed chin, and as she'd done earlier, purred another effective slap. "Hands off, hot stuff. I don't think your wife wants you coming home with fingerprints."

"It's not your fingers I'm interested in." He leaned both forearms on the bar.

She tossed the hand towel she was using to wipe the bar over her shoulder and walked away. Asshole followed her as she moved to the far side of the bar.

Logan sat up a little straighter, his eyes tracking the guy step for step. Years as a Navy SEAL had taught him how to smell trouble a mile away, and this guy smelled rotten. He didn't like the look in the guy's eyes. Logan gripped the edge of the bar and set one foot on the floor.

She called to the bartender at the other end of the bar. "JJ."

JJ looked over. She nodded her head to the side.

Logan had seen her do that earlier, right before she headed to the ladies' room. Apparently so had the asshole who wasn't interested in her fingers. Logan's hands fisted as he rose to his feet. At six foot three, he had a clear view of the dark-haired guy who was still watching her out of the corner of his eye as she headed for the stairs that led down to the bathroom. He felt a strong hand on his wrist and turned, his muscles taut and ready for a fight.

His buddy Dylan Bad narrowed his dark eyes and leaned across the bar. Where the hell had he come from? Logan's eyes slid to the swinging door to the stockroom, still moving from Dylan's entrance.

"Careful with that one, Logan."

He didn't need or want the warning. For a second he wondered if Dylan wanted that sexy little bartender for himself, before remembering that Dylan didn't dip the pen in the company ink, which meant there was something he knew that Logan didn't. *Not for long.* He'd deal with that later.

Logan shot back the same dark stare. "Noted. See the guy trailing her? *He'd* better be careful of *me*." He wrenched his arm free and shook it out. Like a dog with a bone, he headed down the stairs with tunnel vision.

Logan pushed through the throngs of twentysomethings gathered in the stairwell, passing handsy guys with their bodies pressed against scantily clad women and groups talking and drinking while eyeing each other up. The ladies' room was to the left of the staircase, men's to the right. The sassy bartender and the asshole were nowhere in sight. A chill ran down Logan's back. He opened the men's room door, peered inside. The guy wasn't there. Logan's pulse ratcheted up a notch. His muscles corded tighter as he pushed open the women's room door and took an earful of shit from the women inside as he scanned the tight space, coming up empty again. *Motherfucker.*

He pushed through the crowd to the narrow hallway that led to the alley behind the bar. The Emergency Exit Only sign was still hanging loose. *Goddamn Dylan.* The alarm had been broken for a month. He knew Dylan was busy, but at the moment he didn't care. Logan was seeing red as he pushed through the door and heard shuffling and muffled pleas. He stalked down the dark alley, following the sounds. He was upon them before the whites of the bartender's terrified eyes came into focus. Her attacker had her against the wall, trapping her with his hip. One hand fumbled with the waist of her jeans, while the other held her shoulders pressed against the bricks.

Hatred burned in Logan's veins. In one swift move, Logan grabbed the man by the back of his shoulders and tore him off of her.

Her attacker turned. "What the—"

Logan threw him against the brick wall. He crumpled to the ground but got up fast, coming at Logan with his arms flying. Logan was quick, dodging his fists with ease and landing a hard right to the guy's jaw, then a left to his gut. The guy's back met the brick wall with a *thud*.

"Get inside," Logan commanded the bartender as he grabbed the guy's shoulders and threw him down to the pavement, pressing his knee to his sternum.

The idiot tried to get up, but Logan was too powerful, driven by adrenaline and a past filled with too much death. He pinned his arms to the ground with his knees and cocked his fist. The guy's eyes were wide with fear. Blood dripped from his nose and lips. Logan saw the eyes of the men he'd killed on his SEAL missions and the eyes of the man who'd killed his father.

Logan wasn't saving his country, and he knew there was no *saving* his father.

This asshole wasn't worth going to jail for.

"Come into this bar again," Logan seethed, "and you won't walk out."

Chapter Two

STELLA'S BODY TREMBLED so hard her teeth chattered. She'd heard the guy who attacked her scramble away, but she still felt threatened. She couldn't go back into the bar, couldn't do more than stumble a few feet away from where the guy had attacked her. It was all she could do to remember to breathe. She'd seen Kutcher's face, Kutcher's threatening eyes staring back at her as she pleaded for the stranger to stop.

She felt a hand on her arm and jumped, screamed. To her embarrassment, she huddled against the brick wall, her arms pressed close to her chest, hands shielding her face, as if she could become part of the brick wall.

"Shh. It's okay. I'm not the guy who hurt you."

The Midwestern-sounding guy from the bar. He was so tall up close, and broad, which made her cringe closer to the wall.

He held his hands up in surrender, still breathing hard from the fight. "I'm not going to hurt you. I saw him follow you out."

He peered over his shoulder, giving her a second to try to process what had just happened. He'd saved her. Ripped the guy off of her and beat the hell out of him. *Blue eyes from the bar. You saved me.* This repeated in her head several times as she tried to gain control of her senses and force her brain to function again.

"He's gone. He's not going to hurt you anymore." His tone was confident, and she clung to that confidence like a lifeline. "Are you hurt?"

She didn't know, couldn't feel any part of her body. She shook her head, or at least she thought she did. She must have, because relief passed over his face, easing the tension in his jaw.

"I'm going to hold you." It wasn't a question. "Just to let you know you're safe. You're shaking and probably in shock." He gathered her in his strong arms, and she bristled, unable to move. "You're in control. I'll stop if you want me to, but you're safe."

Safe. She didn't know if she'd ever feel safe again.

He tightened the embrace, pressing a hand to the back of her head and splaying his other hand across the width of her back. "You're okay. I won't let anything happen to you. You can tell me to let you go, and I will."

She didn't know if she wanted him to let her go. She wanted to believe that she was safe so badly after being away from everyone she knew and hiding for so long. She needed safety, needed someone to turn to, to talk to. Stella didn't know if it was his words, his confidence, or the way his body cocooned her rather than consumed her. Maybe it was all of those things that allowed tears to finally spill down her cheeks after she'd been brave for months, and her hands to fist in the lapels of his jacket as she accepted his comfort.

"I'm Logan. Logan Wild. Are you sure you're not hurt?" He leaned back a hair, and she pulled him close again, afraid her legs wouldn't sustain her.

"It's okay, sweetheart. I'm not going anywhere," he assured her as he held her close. She soaked his expensive jacket with her tears. Months of repressed sadness, months of proving her strength beyond what she ever thought possible, flooded out of her.

"Thank you," was all she could manage.

"Are you sure you're not hurt? How are you feeling?" he asked again.

It had been months since anyone other than her new boss, Dylan Bad, had cared enough to ask. Her mother would have asked if she'd kept in contact with her. He'd already threatened her mother twice, but her mother had taken out a restraining order, and that seemed to have convinced Kutcher that she was no longer an option for harassment, and he'd returned his focus to Stella. She'd learned the hard way that he knew people. Bad people. People who could trace phone calls and figure out where she was.

Street noises filtered into her ears as the fogginess subsided and her senses returned. She loosened her grip on her savior—*Logan.* "I think I'm okay."

He searched her eyes for what seemed like forever. She wondered if he saw the person she used to be somewhere inside her. She was still there; she knew she was. Somewhere buried below the fear and the fatigue, below the false bravado and the harsh exterior she'd had to project in order to survive. Hopefully one day Stella would find a way to become that person again. But for now she had to figure out this man who an hour ago she thought was too dangerous to talk to. And now? Now she didn't know what to think. He had saved her, comforted her, but Kutcher had been sweet and caring at first, too. Fear needled its way to the surface again, forcing her to push away from Logan.

His brows knitted together. She took a step away, and her back met the bricks again. She winced in pain. It seemed *all* of her senses had returned, and as she gulped in a lungful of the cool night air, she cataloged the pain in her upper back, wrists, and the back of her head. *Great.* This was just what she needed.

"You're hurt."

"I'm fine. Just shaken."

His eyes pierced through her lie with ease as he visually assessed her again, reaching a hand behind her head. She dodged his touch, moving to the right and sending a sharp pain down her neck. She blinked back tears that threatened to weaken her resolve.

He held his hands up again in surrender. "I was just checking for a bump on your head. Maybe I should take you to the hospital. You need to report this to the police."

She shook her head, forgetting about the pain. She winced, and Logan reached a hand toward her, then dropped it, as if he knew she'd pull away. The police would want her real name, and she wasn't taking any chances. She didn't know how Kutcher was tracking her, but he was getting out of jail in four days, and she'd done a good job these last few months of living under his radar. There was no way she was going to lead him to her.

"No. No hospitals. No police."

Those compassionate, confident eyes of his narrowed again, this time with irritation. He turned his head slightly to the right, keeping his wise eyes trained on her. For a second he had the dark and dangerous look of a man who had seen the ugly side of life, and when he turned to face her again, that darkness lightened and somehow turned back to compassion. Stella didn't trust herself enough to decipher what *that* meant.

"No hospitals? No police? Why?"

Did her savior have to be inquisitive, too? Couldn't he just walk away now that he'd taken care of the threat? She didn't really want him to walk away, but she didn't want to be taken to a hospital, either.

"No insurance."

He seemed to buy that—for a second. "The clinic, they'll see you. You have to get checked out."

"I'm fine. Really. Look—"

"Logan."

"Logan." She didn't want to push away the only person who had reached out to her, the man who had put himself in harm's way for her, but she had no choice. The guy who held her captive was nothing next to Kutcher.

"I don't want to go to a clinic or a hospital. Thank you for helping me." Her shoulders dropped a little with the words, with the reality of what could have happened if he hadn't come to her rescue.

"Thank you so much." *Stay strong, strong, strong.* "But I'm fine."

He stepped back and ran his hand though his hair, placed his other hand on his hip, and paced. His shirt was untucked from the fight, his jacket torn at the shoulder, and when he spoke, his tone softened—not at all like the seductive man he'd been in the bar. It was like he'd switched into caregiver mode. How did a person do that? Seductive one minute, savior the next, followed closely with compassion?

"My brother's a doctor. He'll check you out free of charge. Let me at least take you there. Head injuries are never good."

She shook her head, still unwilling to give in and be trapped in a car with him. "I don't even know you."

"What does this have to do—" He held his hands up again. "I'll have him come here to check you out."

The bar. Oh God, my job. Her eyes shot to the door. She'd

been out here so long Dylan must have thought she'd taken off.

Logan scrubbed his face with his hand, and his gaze softened. "Look…I'm a private investigator. I know Dylan Bad, the owner of the bar. I'm not going to kidnap you."

She desperately wanted to trust him. She wanted to trust *someone*. It was exhausting being strong all the time. He'd saved her. He was offering to bring his brother *here* to check her out, *and* he knew Dylan?

"Fine," she relented.

His smile smoothed all his sharp edges. "Good. Great. Let's get you inside, and I'll call my brother Heath. What's your name?"

Stella made a habit of not giving out her real name except when she had to. Dylan knew this about her, as she'd been asked her name many times at the bar. She debated giving her real name to Logan. After all he'd done for her, didn't she at least owe him that?

He draped a protective arm around her shoulders, and she bristled, pulling out from underneath it and eyeing him cautiously. Just because he'd saved her didn't mean she was his to possess. She'd come too far to slip backward.

"Stormy. My name is Stormy Knight."

Chapter Three

LOGAN DIDN'T KNOW what to make of Stormy Knight, but one thing was for sure, she was running from something, or at the very least, hiding from something—or someone. The question was, was she hiding out of fear, or was she hiding because she was on the run from the law? The private investigator in him had his theories, and he was chomping at the bit to do a little investigating. But the man in him had seen that flash of vulnerability beneath the sassy, strong exterior she'd projected in the bar, and it piqued all of his protective urges and something deeper that he couldn't put his finger on.

Logan couldn't stand still. He was barely able to remain trapped in the office in the back of the bar long enough to explain to Dylan what had happened. He had tunnel vision again—and it was aimed at finding the jackass who had attacked Stormy and making sure he never went near her, or any other woman, again.

"That guy you followed to the bathroom?" Dylan's dark eyes turned fierce. Logan had known Dylan since they were kids. They'd gone to school together, as had their siblings. With surnames like "Wild" and "Bad," they were destined to become fast friends, and had remained so throughout the years.

"Yeah. You know him?" Logan paced, eyes locked on Stormy. She had a tight look on her face, arms crossed over her chest. Her hair was tousled, her eyes cold and distant, but beyond that there were no visible scars to reveal the vicious attack she'd just endured. She stood tall, shoulders back, with the same confidence she'd conveyed earlier in the evening, as if she'd compartmentalized the attack and moved past it. Logan knew that moving past something so traumatic could be handled that efficiently only with practice, and that bugged the hell out of him.

"No. Never seen him before." Dylan turned to Stormy. "Jesus, are you okay? How long until Heath gets here?"

"I'm fine. I'm ready to finish my shift," she insisted.

"Like hell you are." Logan didn't have time to soften his tone before the words escaped. "Heath will be here any minute."

"I'm fine, and you're not my father, for God's sake. You saved me, but you don't own me."

Touché. "It's not about owning you. It's about what you've been through."

"I'm fine."

"Whoa, guys." Dylan stretched his hands out between them. "Let's not argue about this. He's right. You can't go back to work after something like that, and, Logan…" He lifted his thick dark brows. "Dude, I'm the boss around here, not you."

Logan scoffed, then steadied his gaze on Dylan. "She needs to report this to the police."

"No. No police." She turned away and mumbled, "Jesus…"

Logan's investigative mind sprang to attention. She wasn't giving away a damn thing, but he intended to find out what she was running from. Logan was good at biding his time. He had a bigger fish to catch before making her even more uncomfortable by pressing her for more information. Besides, he could dig up as much information on her as he wanted to when the time was right.

Ten minutes later Heath arrived. Logan left the room so his brother could examine Stormy in private. He was breathing fire, searching the bar until his eyes landed on the group that was there for the bachelor party. His chest burned with renewed anger. Adrenaline coursed through his veins as he pushed his way through the crowd. He placed one hand tightly on the bachelor's shoulder, and before he guided him away from the others, he leaned in close enough that the guy would hear him but no one else could.

"You're coming with me, and if you say a fucking word, I will make sure you never make it to that wedding." The drunken bachelor opened his mouth, then closed it. Logan led him to the service hallway in the back of the bar, grabbed him by the collar, and slammed him against the wall.

"Hey, man. I didn't do anything." The guy held up his hands.

Logan would feel bad for him if he weren't seething too much to feel. "There was a guy with you. Tall, blond, married. He's gone, wore a black button-down shirt and jeans. Who is he?"

The guy blinked several times, his face scrunched up in confusion. "Mike?"

Logan tightened his grip, heard the material tear, and spoke through gritted teeth. "Last name. Place of work. Now."

"He...Mike Winters. Why? I barely know the guy. Met him at work. He's new." His eyes darted down the hall.

"Where's work?" After getting the name of the financial firm where Mike worked, Logan released the guy's shirt and smoothed it down, then leaned in close again. "He attacked a friend of mine. I suggest you stay away from him and be more choosy with your friends." Logan stalked back to the office.

He knocked on the door. "It's Logan. Is it okay for me to come in?" He didn't want to walk in if Heath was still examining Stormy.

"Yes," Heath said through the door.

At thirty-four, Heath was the oldest of the Wild brothers, followed by Logan, Jackson, and Cooper. It seemed their parents were on the one-child-every-two-years plan. They were a close bunch. A random home burglary and attack on their parents that killed their father and blinded their mother had brought them even closer together in recent years. As Heath glanced up at Logan with a look of concern, Logan pushed thoughts of his parents aside. He couldn't think about that right now.

He watched Heath cleaning the cuts on the back of Stormy's head. His dress shirt was open at the collar, sleeves rolled up. Heath had the hallmark Wild chiseled features and blue eyes that earned them all more women than they could wish for. And though as teenagers their rebellious behavior had earned more focus from teachers than they could avoid, the Wild boys had grown to be well-respected businessmen.

Heath glanced at Logan, pressed his lips together, and arched a brow, giving Logan the *How'd you get into this mess* look.

He didn't bother to shoot him back his icy, *shut up and fix her* stare. He was thankful Heath was there, proving once again that they lived up to their father's creed. *When family calls, you answer.*

"Okay, I think you'll live." Heath removed his rubber gloves, and Stormy blew out a breath.

"Thank you for coming. I told your brother I was fine, but—"

Heath laughed as he packed his medical supplies in his leather bag. "You must not know Logan very well. He did the right thing by having you get checked out. That's quite a laceration and bump you have on the back of your head, and those scrapes on your back are already starting to bruise."

She looked from Logan to Heath. "I can handle a few bruises. What do I owe you?"

Logan noticed her wince as she rose from the chair and reached for her purse. He set a gentle hand on hers and shook his head. "We've got this."

"No charge," Heath said. "Any friend of Logan's is a—"

"Patient of yours?" She smirked.

Heath picked up his medical bag and laughed. "Sometimes, yes. Really, this is nothing. It's good to see my brother, and I'm glad you're okay. Ice the knot on your head, twenty minutes every hour, and, Logan, watch her for any signs of concussion. You've had enough of them to know what to look for."

"Concussion?" Stormy reached up and touched the knot on her head, wincing again.

"I don't think you're in danger of one, but just in case, I feel the need to mention it. You're in good hands with Logan. He knows what to look for."

I wish she was in my hands, but I have a feeling she's going to run like the wind as soon as you leave.

"Well, right now I'm in Dylan's hands. I have to finish my shift." Stormy reached for the doorknob.

Heath shot a curious look to Logan.

"Dylan said you're done for the night," Logan reminded her.

"Dylan isn't the one who needs the paycheck."

"I'll let you two hash this out." Heath embraced Logan and gave him a hard pat on the back.

"Thanks again, bro," Logan said. "See you Sunday?"

"Always." Heath took a business card from his wallet and handed it to Stormy. "Call me if you have any trouble, and take care of those cuts."

Stormy tried to follow him out, but Logan stepped in front of her, shutting the door behind Heath.

"Do you mind?" She worked her jaw from side to side.

"You're not serious. You heard what he said."

"And you heard what I said." She crossed her arms again and reached for the door.

Christ Almighty. Really? What was it about her that made him care? He took out his wallet and fished out a few hundreds.

"What are you doing?" She stepped back, as if he'd offered her money for sex.

"You need the paycheck, and I need you safe and healing. I'm giving you your paycheck. Give me a number."

"You can't buy me." She looked away, her jaw set.

He wanted to take her in his arms and remove the veil of confidence that had her body trembling and her eyes blazing. He couldn't help but reach up and smooth her tangled hair.

"I'm not interested in buying you. What happened to you tonight wasn't normal. It wasn't okay, and it's not something you just kick under the mat and move on from."

She glared at him. "Says the man who's never had to fight for his life." Fear and anger coalesced in her eyes, turning them a shade darker. He was sure she meant to look tough, but it revealed her underlying vulnerabilities and tugged at him again.

He stepped closer, lowered his voice, and couldn't help that it came out as a low growl, filled with intensity from harsh memories. "I fought for my life every day for four years."

Her brows knitted together, her lips parted, but no words came.

"I think you should take tonight off and heal for a few hours. You'll be sore tomorrow, and—"

"I'm not—"

He placed a finger over her lips to silence her. Torture. Pure torture. He didn't know why—wrote it off to a stressful night— but hell if he wasn't fighting the urge to seal his lips over hers and make her *his*.

"Don't. I've seen too much for you to tell me you're not sore. You're sore. Your head is throbbing, your back is pulsing along those deep, long scratches. Your muscles are aching from tensing up, and your mind...Your beautiful, strong mind is going to be exhausted tomorrow after realizing, accepting, and trying to move past what that man *could* have—*would have*— done to you. Save your breath, darlin'." He took a step back, giving her room to make a decision.

"But you're right. I'm not your father, and I certainly don't own you." His eyes slid to the pulse point in her neck and fought the urge to soak in the rest of her. "Not all guys are assholes."

Air left her lungs in a rush of heat. She pressed her lips together, as if she meant to stop it, and pushed past him— heading right back out to finish her shift.

Chapter Four

JESUS CHRIST. DID everything Logan Wild say have to ooze sex? Stella had never met anyone more masculine, more virile. He wasn't frighteningly aggressive, like Kutcher was. No, Logan was a different type of brawn altogether. She could tell by the confidence he possessed, the words he chose, the way his blue eyes darkened and narrowed and his voice took on a guttural quality, that when he pleasured a woman, he didn't just take her; he consumed her. She was trembling from anger and fear, her mind was a whirlwind of chaos, and *still* she got damp when he stepped in so close she could smell his scent and taste the liquor on his breath. She'd had to run out of the room to finish her shift just to remember how to breathe. She'd been on the verge of throwing herself at him and fucking him against the door, on the table, bent over the chair. God, she wanted him—and she felt like a slut for wanting him after what had just happened.

She hated that she felt like a slut for wanting something that other people did all the time without second thoughts. She hated Kutcher for making her afraid. Goddamn it. She felt like she was going to explode, and Mr. Blue Eyes was sitting at the end of the bar the whole fucking time, watching her like she was some precious gem that he had to protect.

I'm not a precious gem.

I'm strong. I've survived this long without a guy taking care of me. I'll be damned if I need it now.

Her shift was over at midnight. She glanced at the clock. In five minutes she'd have made it through one more day. In five minutes she'd be closer to the day Kutcher would be released from jail. In five minutes—four minutes now—she'd have three more days to live her shell of a life before she was forced to start looking over her shoulder again, because he'd appear. Oh yes, of that she had no doubt. Kutcher always appeared. She'd made one big mistake at the last gas station she'd stopped at and mistakenly used her credit card for food. She'd been lucky when he'd been jailed for assaulting the guy at the gas station, but that didn't dull the ache of knowing he'd attacked that poor man because he was looking for her.

She was on borrowed time until the lion would be released to stalk his prey.

Stella went into the back office and grabbed her purse. Dylan turned away from his desk with an irritated look in his dark eyes. He'd been pissed when she'd returned to work, but he'd finally given in and allowed her to finish her shift.

"Stella, do you want a ride home, or is Logan still out there?"

"He's out there."

She lived only a few blocks away, and she was used to walking home with heightened senses, listening for footsteps following too closely, her eyes darting to the alleys as she passed. She hated always being on alert, too, but even though Kutcher was locked up, he'd left a trail of awareness that she couldn't shake. Because of the attack tonight, she was dreading the walk home even more than usual. No matter how many times she played tough, inside she was still that girl from Connecticut who wanted to live a safe, comfortable life. Only now she wanted to live it with that darker side he'd exposed, the side that loved raw sex and visceral, animalistic passion. It scared her as much as it excited her. She knew she couldn't have both. She'd seen the dark side—and it was too dark. But part of her knew that she was no longer the white-fence type of girl. She was stuck in some middle ground she knew nothing about, and it pissed her off just thinking about it.

Fucking Kutcher.

She shouldered her purse and reached for the door, hesitating momentarily under Dylan's steady gaze. Dylan was the only person in her *new life* who knew about Kutcher and what she'd gone through. They'd become friends over the past few weeks. He'd been curious when she'd asked to be paid in cash, and at first he'd flatly turned her down, but before she left the bar that night, he'd given in to her plight of being new in town and needing the cash in order to keep her apartment. It was a lie. She'd had cash saved from when she'd moved, and she had somewhere in the neighborhood of seven thousand, eighty-six dollars left. But she needed the job. Seven thousand dollars didn't go far in New York City.

"That guy Logan? How well do you know him?"

Dylan leaned back in his chair. "If you're asking me if he's like your ex, he's not. He's been through hell and back. He's a good man. You can trust him."

She nodded, feeling slightly more at ease.

The bar closed at two, and there were still throngs of customers milling about. The confidence she wore like a shield while she was behind the safety of the bar thinned as she made her way to the front. Blue Eyes was on his feet and at her side in seconds, one arm on her lower back, eyes darting protectively around them.

"What are you doing?" She kept her eyes trained on the door.

"Making sure you get home okay."

When he pushed the door open, she walked through and kept on going. What was he doing? Stalking her? He fell in step beside her, returning his hand to her lower back. She craved it and feared it at once. She couldn't afford to be stupid, like she'd been when she went to the ladies' room. She should have screamed, kneed that guy in the balls, done something other than panic and flail her useless hands at him.

She stopped and extricated herself from Logan.

"I'm supposed to just let you follow me home?" She crossed her arms, affecting a barrier between them. His eyes warmed and the edge of his lips quirked up in a half smile. He was too damn handsome for his own good. She bet that looks alone got him into bed with many women.

She might be next on that list.

Stop it!

"I'd drive you home, but you made it clear that you're not getting in the car with a stranger. I thought about calling you a cab, but I have the feeling you're not the type of woman to take handouts, and given that you finished your shift because you needed the paycheck, I doubt you want to spend money on cab fare." He shrugged. "I'm a private investigator, not a rapist. That guy who attacked you is still out there, and I want to make sure you get home safely."

She'd been so overwrought with trying to move past what had happened, then getting caught up with Kutcher being released from jail, that she hadn't thought about what might happen *next* with the asshole who'd attacked her. No wonder

Logan's eyes were darting all over. Pride wouldn't let her accept his offer. She wasn't a damsel in distress, and she didn't want to come across as one. Not even to the handsome PI who wanted to protect her. It was probably a game to him anyway. *I am man, big protector; now fuck me good.*

The thought made her smile, because she'd like to do just that.

She spun on her heels and walked away without a word, knowing damn well he'd follow. Which also made her smile, although she gritted her teeth to keep from revealing it.

The long city blocks were never really dark, though they were eerily dim. Even the back streets seemed to be illuminated by the energy of the city. The trees were in full bloom, and for a moment Stella allowed herself to pretend she was back in Mystic, walking to her apartment along the pretty streets, without fear, without a sexy bodyguard whose presence felt much bigger when it was just the two of them in the night. She reveled in the memories of walking along the harbor and wanted desperately to one day be able to return to her hometown and feel safe again. She didn't know if she ever wanted to live there again, but being able to see her mother without looking over her shoulder would be a gift from the heavens above. She couldn't imagine ever having that again.

She couldn't imagine making it back to Mystic alive once Kutcher was released from jail. He was the epitome of an abuser—overly apologetic and manipulative. Like all the other mind-fucked women who stay with abusers, she'd fallen for his ploys and had taken him back after the first few times, but when she'd finally broken things off, he'd become the worst kind of stalker, appearing out of nowhere and attacking her. If he couldn't have her, he didn't want anyone else to have her either.

She found out too late that he'd been at the party where she met him because he was selling drugs to one of the wealthy guests. She hadn't realized how big his drug-dealing business was until she'd made the mistake of telling him she knew about his operation. That was when he'd turned from leaving bruises to wanting her dead.

When they turned onto her street, Stella felt Logan move closer, tension surrounding him like a bubble; he felt dense and powerful. She didn't live in the best neighborhood. As they walked around that final corner and headed down the deserted sidewalk, the sounds of cars and people gave way to eerie silence, with the random dog barking in the distance. She was fully aware of the moment she shed the false security that city nightlife provided and her armor clicked into place. She knew that all it took was one night, such as tonight, where in the midst of a crowded bar, evil could pick a target and make its move, and no one would be the wiser.

She shot a glance at Logan—jaw clenched, eyes narrow and scrutinizing, fists at the ready.

No one but Logan Wild.

"This is it," she said as they came to the alley that led to the back of the row house where she rented a room. She took a step toward the alley, and he gently grabbed her arm, then stepped ahead of her, leaving no room for negotiation. He was paving the way. Ensuring her safe arrival.

She'd never met anyone like Logan before. Even the guys she'd grown up with, the ones who'd known her from the time she was a schoolgirl and had told her that they'd be there for her when they first heard about what Kutcher was doing, had abandoned her. Fear was a powerful thing. They'd acted as if bad luck were contagious. Her friends had all put space between them in the final days before she'd left town. Only that poor man at the gas station where she'd mistakenly stopped and used her credit card for food had tried to stand up to Kutcher. She'd learned on the news that he'd ended up in the hospital. The upside was that Kutcher had landed in jail for a few months; the downside was that the poor gas station attendant had spent weeks healing from broken ribs and lacerations. She still carried that guilt around her neck like a noose. She hadn't even been able to thank him because she feared that making contact would give Kutcher a fresh scent to follow.

She unlocked the door, and Logan put an arm out in front of her, blocking her path.

"I'll check it out first."

She rolled her eyes at his insistence but couldn't deny the relief of knowing someone else would endure that first few seconds of *what if* instead of her. That steady panic that grew every night when she walked home and then first stepped foot into her basement apartment.

"Be my guest." She tried to sound as if she didn't care, then held her breath as he walked into her apartment and flicked on the lights.

Logan didn't seem to possess the same fear that had sent her friends scattering from her life. What would it be like to be that self-assured? She followed him into the small kitchen and watched as he stepped around the small table and two chairs, then opened the pantry. The kitchen was no bigger than most people's bathrooms, but it was functional, and she didn't need extravagance.

Logan glanced at her, forced a smile, but she could see he was in protection mode. His eyes were narrowed and serious, and his shoulders had risen with tension. He planted his legs with every measured step, reminding her of a panther, stealthy and powerful, the way he moved through the small hallway, checked out the bathroom, then the laundry closet on the opposite wall. He methodically checked out every nook and cranny in her apartment. She moved closer as he stepped into the bedroom. With no doorway to separate the two, he had a clear view of her double bed, single dresser, and the clothes hanging in her closet. When she'd run from Mystic, she'd taken only what she could carry without assistance. She'd fit everything she needed in one suitcase and two backpacks. Stella had fretted about having enough clothes to sustain whatever job she'd eventually find to hold her over, but she'd quickly realized that it wasn't clothes, shoes, or other material items that she needed in order to get through each day. She'd learned that strength and determination were the only *must haves* she needed in order to survive.

What Stella missed most was hearing her mother's laugh, seeing the happiness in her eyes when Stella walked through the door to visit, and the way her mother lowered her voice when she talked about something she found funny or interesting. God, she missed her. She glanced at the picture of her mother on the bedside table, the only material thing she owned that she really cared about.

"I think you're all clear." The sleeves of his dress shirt were pushed up to his elbows, exposing muscular forearms with a dusting of dark hair. The top buttons were still undone, tails untucked. The fight had added streaks of dirt to his shirt and a wild messiness to his hair, making him even more devastatingly handsome.

If Logan had been standing in her bedroom looking like sex on legs before Kutcher, Stella might have tried to flirt with him.

She wouldn't have thought about seducing him before Kutcher, because before Kutcher, she was a good girl, and her seductive ways included little more than stolen glances. Kutcher ruined that for her. Ruined her. Thinking of all the ways Kutcher had changed her, and the things he'd stolen from her, brought anger. It started deep inside her, simmering, brewing, bubbling up in her chest, until she wanted to scream.

She took a step closer to Logan, thinking about when he'd first come into the bar. His eyes had locked on hers, inciting fear, then desire.

"Thank you. There aren't many places to hide in here." She shifted her eyes to the bed, felt her cheeks flush at the pang of longing to be touched that gripped her, and turned away from Logan. She shouldn't be thinking about lying on the bed beneath him, feeling him move inside of her, but wasn't that a normal thing for a girl to think around someone who looked like him and acted so nice? Kutcher had slithered into her psyche and coated the most normal thoughts with guilt and fear.

"Hey, you okay?" He came up behind her, so close she'd bump into him if she moved. Warm hands touched her arms, and she closed her eyes, fighting images of Kutcher doing that exact same thing, then slamming her into a wall. In an instant, anger reared up inside her again.

Logan's hand slid down her arm as he came around and faced her. "Your whole body just went rigid. Did I hurt you?"

As Stella shook her head, she realized that while she'd been fantasizing about Logan, her pain had subsided. "No."

"Why did you flinch?"

He was so close she saw every sliver of whisker along his jaw.

"Did I scare you?" His voice slid over her skin, warming her all over.

"No. You didn't scare me. I'm just mad." She didn't know where the confession had come from, but it opened a door inside her and her breaths came faster, harder. His eyes were seductive, and she wanted to see them staring down at her while he was buried deep inside her, taking away her pain and fear and filling her with pleasure.

"I'm sick of being afraid." She turned away to distract herself from the lust coiling down low in her belly. "I'm tired of measuring every thought. Every move."

"Stormy…" He came up behind her again. The air around them blazed with heat. "That's not your real name—we both know that."

She took a step away, half expecting Logan to grab her arm and spin her around, the way Kutcher would have. But he didn't. He pinned her with an empathetic look from a few feet away, and she felt her armor start to crack.

She'd just been attacked. She should be *more* fearful, afraid to climb out from under all that armor and let go, but she felt just the opposite. She was sick and tired of the weight of running. She wanted to reclaim her life, her body, her mind.

She was powerless to stop the truth from spilling out. "I want to walk down the street without my heart hammering and my nerves on fire." Her arms swept through the hall as she paced, breathing like there wasn't enough oxygen in the room. "I can't even use my real name. I want to be able to go home and visit my mother without worrying that some psycho is going to attack and kill me."

"Why can't you do those things?" His tone was tender, yet serious.

She scoffed and closed the distance between them, drawn to

the caring look in his eyes, the way his hands had unclenched and reached for her. "All I want is to be a regular girl." She took a step back, battling her desires. He took a step closer. Her chest rose and fell with each angry breath, nearly grazing his. She wanted that contact, wanted to feel her breasts pressed against his strong chest.

"You know the worst part about all of this?"

"Tell me why you can't do those things, and I'll figure out the worst part." His eyes went nearly black as his hands skimmed her arms again, sending a shiver down her spine.

"Ugh!" She tried to walk away, and he held her still with little more than a touch of his fingertips. She didn't *want* to get away.

"Tell me. I'll help." He was dead serious.

"You can't help. No one can help. I'll never be normal again. I'll never be able to do any of those things, or walk down the street without fear, or fuck any goddamn guy I want without worrying about being killed."

His eyes searched hers. "I'm not going to kill you. But I'm willing to help with all those things, and God knows I'll happily fuck you until you can't remember your name."

His potent virility made the room feel smaller, hotter. Her limbs trembled, and tears stung her eyes, which only pissed her off even more. She lifted her chin in challenge.

"Is that what you want, Stormy? You want me to take you right here? To spread your legs wide, lick your pussy until you come over and over again, then stick my hard cock inside you and fuck you until you forget everything else in the world? Because I promise you, Stormy Knight, you'll not only forget how to think, but you'll be so sore tomorrow that every step you take will remind you of me filling you so completely that you'll crave more."

His eyes dropped from her face, to her neck, to her breasts, lazily appraising her with a maddening hint of arrogance that made her desire spike. She was already wet with need, and when he cupped her breast and brushed his thumb over her taut nipple, she lost any sense of right and wrong and gave in to the smoldering flames between them.

"God, yes—"

It came out in one long breath, which he captured in his mouth as he sealed his lips over hers, his tongue thrusting deep and hard as he claimed her. His hands were on fire as he tore at her shirt and threw it to the floor. She was too ready, too greedy, couldn't wait to see the muscles that had saved her, that had protectively stalked her apartment. She grabbed both sides of his shirt and ripped with all her might. Buttons scattered. Logan laughed, a guttural, lustful laugh as he kissed a path down her neck and grazed his teeth over her collarbone and ground his hard length against her. She gave in to the need that had been buried for months and fumbled with the buttons on her jeans while he tore her bra from her body and took one of her breasts in his mouth. Forget the jeans, she buried her hands in his hair, holding him to her as he sucked and licked and tortured her hard nipple, sending heated anticipation between her legs.

"Oh God, Logan. It's been so long."

One strong hand rubbed her through her jeans. Her head tipped back with the delicious friction as he stroked her pussy and sucked her breast, driving her out of her fucking mind. More. She needed more. She was so wet, so close to the edge. She tugged at her jeans, needing them off. Logan made quick work of stripping her bare.

He sank to his knees and spread his hands on her thighs, then looked up at her. "Holy fuck, you're gorgeous. You're sure? I'm not forcing, I'm not—"

"Yes. Yes. God yes."

She thrust her hips forward, and he obliged with vigor. Lord, did he oblige. His talented tongue swirled and stroked while his fingers rubbed her clit with deadly precision. She'd forgotten how good it felt to get lost in pleasure. Ripples of ecstasy rolled through her, taunting her. The orgasm was just out of reach. He took her clit between his teeth, and she cried out.

"I'll stop."

He was too goddamn careful.

"No! I want this." She panted for breath. "Take me, Logan. Whatever I say, it's okay. I want this. I want you."

"Safe word. Red."

Was he fucking for real? It's not like he was tying her up and whipping her.

"I *don't* need a safe word."

"*I* do. You were attacked tonight. I need to know you have the power to stop me. I hear that word, I'll stop. That's my promise to you."

She leveled him with a seductive narrow-eyed stare so he wouldn't misunderstand. "Thank you, Boy Scout. Now please fuck me like you've never fucked anyone before."

He thrust his fingers deep inside her, and she closed her eyes, luxuriating in exquisite pain and pleasure as his teeth found the sensitive bundle of nerves again. The tug of desire had her insides reaching for more as he probed and sucked and licked, turning her entire body into liquid heat, burning, aching. She felt her sex swell, craving more, just as he'd promised. She slammed her eyes shut. It had been so long since she'd felt these overwhelming sensations that her body wanted to remain in the heightened state, to revel in it. He did something incredible with his tongue, and her body surrendered to the molten desire. He lingered over her swollen sex, lapping, taking, keeping her at the peak until a tortured moan escaped her lips. Logan reared up and captured her cries in his mouth. He tasted of her, salty and sweet, as he claimed her mouth, then lifted her into his arms and carried her to the bed, where he devoured her, deepening the kiss as if he were memorizing the curve of every tooth. Their tongues found a rough, needy rhythm as he ground his cock against her, and the gritty fabric of his pants sent her reeling over the edge again.

She tugged and pushed at his jeans, needing him inside her. He stripped quickly and—holy mother of all things sexy, his body was a work of art. Planes of hard, muscular flesh stood before her. Broad shoulders led to a narrow waist, and sinfully sexy ripped abs ended in a thick, hard cock, a bead glistening on the tip. She licked her lips and moved to the edge of the bed, wrapping her fingers around his thick length. He had the most beautiful cock, with a nice, thick, round head, in perfect proportion to the hard, smooth shaft. She licked the wetness from the tip, earning herself a heady groan. His fingers fisted in her hair as she swirled her tongue over the head, then took him in deep. She stroked him hard and fast. His thighs flexed, and his hips thrust forward. She drew him out slowly and licked the base, then focused on his tight sac, earning her a growl that came from deep in his throat.

"Suck my cock," he ground out.

She took him in again, working him with tight strokes. The tip met the back of her throat time and time again.

"That's it. Fuck, that's good."

He guided her efforts, fisting her hair as his hips thrust faster. He grew impossibly bigger, and she knew he was close to release. She quickened her pace, wanting to pleasure him.

"Stop. I'm gonna come, and I want to be inside you."

She drew him out slowly, cradling his balls and causing his head to tip back again. Torturing Logan made her feel empowered, and when his head dropped forward, his eyes nearly black, the look in them made her feel more desired than ever before.

"Can you come more than once?" *Please tell me you can.*

"Can you make me?"

She loved a challenge. Never had, until Kutcher had pushed her past her comfort zone. She forced thoughts of him away, unwilling to allow him to ruin any more of her night.

"Touch yourself while I fuck your mouth, darlin'. I want to see you come with me."

What kind of skill did it take to say *darlin'* and *fuck your mouth* in the same breath and make it sound like his big, strong arms were wrapped around her as he gazed into her eyes? It was like being fucked hard but feeling loved, and she'd never felt anything like it—and didn't want it to end. She reached between her legs, and for a moment she had to close her eyes against the overwhelming sensations. She needed this release, this freedom from living with fear every minute of the day, and with just four days left before Kutcher got out of jail, she wasn't going to miss a second of this gift she'd given herself. This time with Logan.

He grabbed the back of her head and guided her mouth around him, driving his hips forward as she stroked herself to the edge. He filled her mouth so completely she could barely breathe, heightening her pleasure. Tension wound around the backs of her thighs. The muscles in her back flexed as the orgasm coiled around her body like a snake, constricting, alighting every nerve, until it finally claimed her, pulsating tight and fast just as he groaned and thrust his cock deeper, spurting hot streams of salty semen down her throat. He held her head still as he rode the wave of his release, until she'd milked him dry, and his head fell forward with a loud exhalation.

He opened his eyes just as she licked her lips.

LOGAN KNELT BEFORE Stormy, his hands on her knees, and looked deeply into her eyes. He'd been with enough women to know she was using sex as an escape, just as *he* had for so many years. Being one of the US Navy's elite SEAL team had taken his full concentration and total dedication, because Logan didn't believe in just being good at anything. He believed in being the best at everything he did. That didn't end with his profession. It carried over to relationships, sex, and even friendships. That's why he'd never settled down with just one woman. He'd never met anyone whom he wanted to be the best for, and as he gazed into Stormy's eyes and saw relief cloud over, hardening her beautiful features, he felt something in his chest crack open.

He gathered her in his arms and held her close, kissed her cheek, and whispered, "You're amazing, but I just want to hold you." *Hold you? What the hell?* It was her vulnerability that took his emotions to a place they'd never been. She was trying so hard to be strong, to be whatever she felt she needed to be. He wanted to know what or who would put so much fear into this beautiful woman.

Her body was rigid against him, but he wasn't about to let her go. He couldn't allow her to slip right back into that steel vault she kept herself trapped in. He came down on the bed beside her and pulled her up with him, his knee between her thighs, his arms circling her body so he could feel her erratic heartbeat against him.

"Whatever you're running from, let's not think about it right now. Put it aside. For tonight, you're safe." He felt tension, fatigue, and so much unwanted emotion pent up in her that he wanted to give her a break. One night of peace, just like he and his brothers took turns trying to give their mother every night of the week. The feeling of safety, of knowing no one would ever hurt her again. When his mother had been attacked, and his father killed, Logan's life had changed. He'd been protecting his country when the attack had happened, when he should have been home protecting the people he loved most.

"Just fuck me, Logan. Do it so we're both satisfied. Then you can go back to your life. Just give me this one night." Her words were hard but full of need, as if she were challenging herself as well as him.

"I will, babe. Just be with me a minute. Let yourself relax." He didn't know what was going on inside of him, but for the first time in his life he didn't want a quick fuck. He knew the minute he walked out that door, Stormy would consume his thoughts. He'd worry about her. How could he not? With eyes that cut straight to the center of his chest, pleading and arguing in equal measure.

She laughed against his chest. "Relax? That's not going to happen, so either fuck me or leave."

He pulled back then and searched her eyes. "Do you really want me to leave?"

"No. I want you inside me so I can forget my life for another few minutes."

"Babe, I can last longer than a few minutes, but how about first I hold you until you realize you can trust me? I'm really not into fucking people who don't trust me."

"Really? You came in my mouth pretty easily."

She had him there. "Touché. What do you have against relaxing?"

"When you relax, bad things can happen." She pushed away, and he pulled her closer again, smoothed her hair away from her face, and kissed her forehead.

"Not while I'm around."

"So...what? You want me to relax, then have sex with you?"

He shrugged. "Sure. Or relax and don't. Whatever."

She cocked her head to the side, and he wondered how many men had hurt her, how many had treated her like shit. She touched her fingertip to the roundish scar on the right side of his chest, then traced the fine white line that ran along his ribs to the next, like she was connecting the dots.

"What happened?" She gazed up. Her brows knitted together, and he could see she was softening toward him again.

He shrugged. "I only give that out on a need-to-know basis, but I'd be willing to swap an answer for an answer."

He didn't like to talk about his scars, and he didn't like to talk about his time with the SEALs. It reminded him too much of the man he'd lost while he was gone. His father had tried so hard to talk him out of becoming a SEAL. *It's dangerous. You're too smart to spend your life getting shot at. Stay home, buddy boy.* But Logan had something to prove, though he never knew whom he was proving it to other than himself. He'd won the Silver Star, the Purple Heart, the Combat Action Ribbon, and a few more awards, but nothing would make up for fighting for someone else's life while his parents were fighting for their own. He didn't regret protecting his country, but he regretted not being around for his family when they needed him most, and he swore he'd never put anyone above those he loved again.

"Okay," she whispered. "You first. How did you get this scar?" She pressed her lips to the scar on his chest.

"Bullet wound. I was a Navy SEAL. It was a night mission. I got four of their guys. They got one lucky shot. Then I killed two more." He watched her process the information. Her eyes dropped to the scar, and her finger slid lightly over it.

"Were you scared?"

He hadn't even known he'd been shot until he'd lost so much blood that he could no longer pull the trigger on his gun. He'd been in the midst of combat. Adrenaline had dulled his ability to feel pain and heightened his ability to perform.

"Only of not seeing my family again." He'd never admitted that to anyone, and as the words came, a lump formed in his throat. "Who are you running from?" he asked to distract himself from the painful memory.

She shook her head, closed her eyes.

"Okay." He softened his voice, understanding just how deep her wounds went. "Are you running from the law, or for your life?"

She lay on her back and stared up at the ceiling. He watched the skin on her neck pull tight as she swallowed.

"*For* my life." A whisper.

A whisper that cut like a knife.

Logan lay on his side. He slid his knee up over her thighs and curled his left arm around her head, then leaned in close so his body blanketed the left side of hers, and he pressed his hand to her cheek, holding her face to his chest. He didn't say anything at first. He wanted her to feel safe. His mother hadn't wanted to share her fear with her sons after the attack that left her blind. Late one night Logan had relentlessly pursued the truth, peppering her with questions, and when she'd finally told him how she'd been too scared to call out for help and his father had risen from bed and charged the menacing burglar without fear—and the stranger had shot him twice in the chest, then savagely beat her, leaving her blind and barely breathing—he'd seen the fear come rushing back. That was three years ago, and Logan knew that although her fear had lessened, it would never fully disappear.

"Why?" he finally asked.

"I made a bad choice in a boyfriend."

"What has he done to you?"

He felt wetness on his fingers and looked down at the tears slipping from her eyes. He brushed them away with his thumb and pressed his lips to her forehead. Seeing her like this made his chest feel tight and achy. It was an unfamiliar feeling, but somewhere in the back of his mind he remembered feeling this way when his mother had confided in him. Anger born from the memory of his mother's tears began to replace the ache.

"Your turn," she whispered as she stroked his cheek.

Stormy's voice brought him back from the memory.

Her hand was soft and warm, and her touch was tender as she ran a finger along his jaw, down his neck to his chest, hesitating for a few seconds at the scar over his right pec. She followed the thin white scar that mapped a path to the second, lower patch of marred skin. "This? Did you get it while you were a SEAL?"

He opened his mouth to lie, but no words came. He was

usually so good at avoiding intimate questions. When women asked about his scars, he shrugged and said, *Life's a bitch. Sometimes it leaves scars.* He didn't want to feed Stormy that line. She was sharing her secrets, and he felt compelled to share his.

"No," he admitted.

She pressed her palm to the scar and held his gaze. "How, then?"

His breathing came harder as the night he'd tracked down his parents' attacker came back to him and played like a horror movie in his head. He wanted to run from the memory, from the tightening in his chest. He wanted to forget the way they'd had to pry him off the man's limp body as he pummeled him with his fists while blood poured from the bullet wound in his gut.

He gazed down at Stormy again and saw the softening of the walls that had separated them only moments ago, and he wanted in.

"Getting a bad guy out of the way."

"Did you get shot?" She pressed closer to him, as if she thought he needed to be comforted more than she did.

"Yes." He tried to caress the tension lines from her cheek, but the more her eyes scrutinized him, the more pronounced they became.

"Were you scared?"

He dropped his head between his shoulders and closed his eyes for a beat.

"Terrified." The admission felt like a thousand pounds had fallen from his shoulders.

"Of dying?" she whispered.

"No." He raised his eyes to hers. "Of dying before I killed

him."

She stared at him then for a long time, and the air between them didn't heat with passion the way it had been doing since they met, but it shifted. In those few seconds Logan felt his world tilt, their answers tethering them together. When she lifted her head and pressed her lips to his, he let her control the intensity, pulling her closer, wanting more of her, but not wanting to put any more fear into her head than she already had. She kissed him tenderly, planting soft kisses along his lower lip. He closed his eyes and lowered himself to his back, wanting, needing to be touched. She pressed her hands to his cheeks and slanted her lips over his, deepening the kiss, until it felt like salvation. She kissed him hungrily, and he met her efforts, as if they each could provide redemption to the other. Him from his past, her for a future. He couldn't hold back. He wanted to claim that redemption, to claim her as his own. In one swift move he swept her beneath him and spread her legs with his knees, the tip of his arousal pressed against her swollen, wet flesh.

"Condom," he breathed against her lips.

"I'm on the pill."

He knew he should be worried about STDs, but he wasn't. For the first time in his life sex felt like more than just a release, and he wanted to feel every bit of her velvety heat. He wanted to possess the woman who'd kissed him like he was hers—and damn did he want to be hers.

But he needed her to have peace of mind.

"I'm clean, Stormy. Tested religiously every thirty days."

"Fuck me, Logan."

That stopped him cold, and he drew back, pinning her to the mattress with his eyes alone. "No."

Disappointment flashed in her eyes. *Disappointment.* Not fear, not annoyance. He knew this was different for her, too.

"I want to make love to you."

Her mouth dropped open, and for a moment he thought he'd fucked up, misread everything.

"Yes," she whispered. She pressed on the back of his hips, guiding his throbbing cock inside her.

He pushed in until he was buried to the hilt, then stilled at their first joining. Her lips curled up in a smile, and for the first time, her smile reached her eyes. His chest grew tight at the look in her eyes, a different type of tightening than anger or regret, and he never wanted to lose this feeling. He sealed his lips over hers as they moved in perfect sync. Her hips met his deep, slow thrusts. He was in no hurry to find his release. Logan kissed her jaw, her neck, settled his teeth over her shoulder and bit down, earning him a sexy moan. Her hips bucked off the mattress. He laced his fingers with hers, holding her hands beside her head so he could gaze into her eyes as her body swallowed his hard length time and time again. Her body arched toward him. Her soft curves molded to his strength. The warmth of her soft flesh was intoxicating.

"Logan…" A heady whisper.

"Am I hurting you?"

She shook her head, nibbled her lower lip. "You feel incredible. So big. So…good." Her eyes filled with lust, surprise, and unfathomable beauty. "I'm going to…."

With his next thrust, she slammed her eyes shut. Her legs flexed, and her fingernails dug into the backs of his hands.

"That's it, darlin'. Come for me. Come for us."

Her eyes flew open, and he saw confusion in her gaze, and hell if he wasn't confused, too, but he felt *something*, and he wasn't about to ignore it. He didn't know if he'd ever feel it again.

He sealed his mouth over hers, grinding his hips in a circular motion, stroking all the nerves that kept her at the peak of her release, until she tore her mouth away with the need for air. Seeing her in the heat of ecstasy, her lips parted, eyes closed, hair spread out around her, was too much. A fine sheen of sweat between her breasts met his chest as he thrust deeper. He was lost in the pulsing heat around his cock, as they spiraled over the edge together, clawing for purchase wherever they could grab hold. Her legs locked around his waist as she mewed into his mouth, tightening around him, unwilling to set him free. Not that he wanted to be freed. Hell no. He was exactly where he wanted to be, buried deep inside the woman who finally made him feel again.

Chapter Five

LOGAN STOOD IN front of his mother's house in the early hours of the morning. He didn't like to think about his family's tragedy, but sometimes thinking about it was all he could do. Memories crept up on him at strange times, and last night Stormy had stirred memories that made him want to go back and live parts of his life over. If only he'd been around when his parents had been attacked. He'd saved the lives of a woman and three children while he was out on a mission that very weekend in Afghanistan. He remembered the wide eyes of the little seven-year-old boy and the screams of his two- and three-year-old sisters, who were huddled against his frail body. He'd yelled at Logan in his native tongue, turning his back to him and shielding his baby sisters, ready to protect them with his life—*at seven*—while his mother lay bleeding two feet away. At that moment, as Logan sealed the room as best he could and then went back out to eliminate the remaining Taliban that had stormed the Pushkin village, Logan felt like he was doing the right thing. He was saving lives, protecting his country. What he hadn't learned until later was that while he was saving strangers, his father lay dying in a pool of blood on his bedroom floor. Shot while trying to shield his wife from a burglar.

Logan shoved his hands into his pockets and bowed his head. When he'd left Stormy, he'd gone home and showered and tried to sleep, but sleep had evaded him. He couldn't shake the fear he'd heard in her voice, or how similar she'd sounded to his own mother when she'd finally relayed that awful night to him.

He walked the perimeter of the old bungalow-style home. His mother had refused to move after the attack, which had driven him and his brothers nearly insane. They'd grown up in the small two-story home. Their parents' bedroom was on the first floor in the back of the house. Logan and Heath had shared a small bedroom at the top of the stairs. They'd had bunk beds, like Jackson and Cooper had in the loft. That was all that would fit in the small bedroom. The closet served as their dresser, while Jackson and Coop kept their clothes in a pint-sized dresser in the loft. They had years of good memories in that old house—and now they were overshadowed by one terrible night.

Logan checked the locks on the windows as he made his way around to the back door. The old stairs leading to the door creaked, and he hoped his mother and her supersonic hearing didn't wake from the noise. He checked the lock on that door and peered into the kitchen. Even blind, his mother somehow managed to keep the house spotless, as if she'd spent the thirty years she'd been living there before losing her sight memorizing every counter, every hallway, every nook and cranny of the place.

A light flicked on down the hall, and he knew he'd woken her. Damn. She still hit the lights when she woke up, a force of habit at this point. He hadn't wanted to scare her. He waited until she shuffled out of the bedroom in her ancient housecoat to call out to her and unlock the door. He worried about frightening her, but Mary Lou Wild had a sixth sense when it came to her sons. She sensed each of them before they announced themselves. Logan would bet she'd known it was him standing on the porch before she'd left her bedroom, but he wasn't taking any chances.

"It's Logan, Ma." He watched a smile form on her lips. Her hand trailed along the wall as she made her way into the kitchen. Logan unlocked the door and walked inside.

"Logan." She never failed to sound happy to see him, even at five thirty in the morning.

He folded her in his arms and kissed her cheek. "I'm sorry to wake you, Ma. I was just..." He shrugged, knowing she couldn't see it, but also knowing she'd somehow sense it. From what she'd told Logan, she'd sensed something ominous coming and had told their father she felt uneasy, though she didn't know why. It wasn't until hours later, when she awoke with a start and found the man entering their bedroom, that she understood her earlier apprehension. Her gasp had awoken her husband, Bill, and he'd leaped from the bed like a true hero, ready to take on whatever had scared the woman he adored. And adored he did, every minute of every day. The family hadn't had much while the boys were growing up. Mary Lou had stayed home with them, taking on seamstress work from the dry cleaner's down the road for extra income, and Bill had worked at a factory. But Logan and his brothers had never wanted for anything. They'd had loving parents who'd demanded they do well in school and pinched pennies to help pay for their college.

His father lost his life for some asshole's selfish decision to burglarize their home. He'd gotten away with a small stash of jewelry, including his father's family ring, an old DVD player, a television, a few pieces of silver—and their family's heart and soul. Logan's father's life.

Logan would never forget that his father had given his all for his children. He only wished he'd been there to give his all for his father in return. He was making up for it now. He and his brothers took turns looking after their mother, stopping by each day to ensure she had groceries, to help her with meals, care for her lawn, and take her wherever she needed or wanted to go. And on Sundays they all got together at her house for a family dinner. Everything they did was out of love for their parents, not out of pity. Save for Logan, whose love was topped off with guilt.

"Sweetheart, what are you doing here so early? Are you okay?" She ran her fingers over his face, and Logan held his breath. His mother would know in seconds exactly where his mind was. There was no hiding from her. She might not be able to see, but her fingers had some kind of emotion sensors. They didn't miss a damn thing.

"You're tense." She reached out beside her until she felt a chair, and she pulled it out from the table. "Sit, lovey. I'll make you some tea."

"Ma, you don't have to do that." He didn't try to stop her because he knew it would do no good. She doled out love through tea and talks, always had. And right then, maybe he needed a little comfort more than he cared to admit.

"*Tsk*. Sit, baby." She moved with the familiarity of sight, pulling mugs from the cabinets and setting the kettle on the stove. She must have heard Logan walking to the pantry to retrieve the tea, and she waved him off. "I've got it. Please, baby, sit."

He smiled as he sank into a wooden chair. *Baby, lovey, sweetie.* She rarely used their given names. He'd long ago given up on claiming not to be a baby. He and his brothers knew that to her, no matter how big or how old they were, she'd always dote on them as if they were youngsters.

She set their tea on the table and settled into a chair beside him with a sigh.

"I'm sorry I woke you, Ma. I was just checking things out."

"Logan, baby, you don't have to do that at all hours. That was a crazy onetime thing. I'm fine. Lord knows you and your brothers make sure of that every day." She patted her dark hair. She'd always been pretty, and even though she looked as though she'd aged ten years since his father's death, she was still beautiful. The fine lines around her eyes told of her age, or maybe of her loss, but her olive complexion and once blue, now slate gray eyes gave her a Mediterranean look. Although Mary Lou was about as far from Mediterranean as a woman could get. His parents had met when his mother still lived in Weston, Colorado, where she'd grown up on her family's ranch. His father had grown up in Trusty, Colorado, not far from Weston. He'd been working as a trucker and had stopped in at the diner in Weston where Mary Lou happened to be sitting at the counter alone, waiting for a girlfriend to meet her for lunch. His father had spent the next few months wooing her. Seven months after they met, they'd married and moved to New York, where Bill had been offered a more stable position with no travel. Logan's mother always said that he had a little bit of his father's Weston charm in him.

He sipped his tea. "How are you, Mom? Heath is coming by tonight to take you out to the market."

"Yes, Heath's a good boy. He told me about your friend."

"Did he?"

"You know Heath. He likes to fill me in. He said he saw something in the way you looked at her." She lifted her eyes to his, and even though he knew she couldn't see him, he felt as though she saw right through him. He'd never been able to lie to her, not as a kid, when lying would have saved him from being grounded, and not as an adult, when it might have saved him from a lecture or two.

At least, he'd never been able to tell her an outright lie. He'd never told her that he'd killed the man who'd attacked her and killed his father, but he'd told her that she was safe and the guy had been taken care of. Had she asked if he'd killed him, Logan would have answered truthfully, but she never had.

He'd tracked the bastard down using the contacts he'd made as a private investigator and had tailed him until he had a chance to nail him. Logan had caught him casing a house and had reported it to the police, but the police weren't all they were cracked up to be. They didn't make it in time. The woman's scream drew him into the house with one goal in mind—making sure that asshole never hurt another person. He'd completed that mission with a mixture of pride, guilt, and remorse, and that strange baggage had remained a constant companion ever since.

He pushed those thoughts away when his mother's hand covered his.

"Lovey, what is it? You seem conflicted."

"How do you do it, Ma? How do you know what's in my head?" He'd asked her a hundred times before and knew he'd ask her a hundred more, because her non-answer was always the same.

"I'm your mother. Mothers know these things."

He lifted her hand to his lips and pressed a soft kiss to it. "I love you, Mom."

"I love you, too, dear, but you're avoiding my question."

He laughed, sipped his tea. "You never did let me off the hook easy."

"What good would that have done? We own our feelings in this family, Logan, and it seems to me that it's been ages since you had any feelings toward a woman to own."

Logan shifted uncomfortably in his seat. "She's running from a guy."

"Oh, Logan." She pressed her lips together and shook her head. "And that's got your heart all tied up in knots. You're a savior at heart, sweetheart. That's why you fought your father so hard to join the navy. You always needed to be saving someone. He was so proud of you."

Tears stung Logan's eyes while guilt settled heavy and hard like lead in his gut. There was a time he wouldn't have believed his father was proud of him because of the way he'd argued with Logan about his desire to join the military. But in his heart, and now a world away from his rebellious youth, Logan understood that his father hadn't wanted to risk losing him. He knew now that his father had always been proud of him.

"Be careful, Logan." She'd called him by his name several times, which meant she wanted him to listen carefully to what she was saying. "Some women are magnets for trouble. They thrive on drama, never really looking for an escape, but rather putting themselves in harm's way. Damsels in distress and all that. While others find themselves in a bad situation and do everything within their power to find their way free from the nightmare. It's the latter that are worthy of your love."

"I'm not talking love, Ma."

"Mm-hmm." She sipped her tea with a soft nod.

He hated when she did this, acted as if she listened to what he said but knew better.

"Ma, really."

She patted his hand again. "Okay, lovey. Where are you headed so early in the morning?"

He clenched his jaw. He was heading over to have a *talk* with the guy who'd attacked Stormy last night—Mike Winters—to ensure he'd never go near her, or near NightCaps again. He'd done a quick search on the guy when he'd gotten home. Married, two kids, stay-at-home wife. A little threat of exposure should nip him in the bud. But he wasn't going to burden his mother with that knowledge. The minute she found out he was protecting Stormy, she'd say he was already stepping in too deep.

Maybe he was, but he didn't have to admit it.

"Work."

She raised her brows in that *uh-huh* way she had. "Okay, well, you be careful at *work*, and remember what I said. Metal to magnet is dangerous."

Logan always felt lighter after seeing his mother, and today was no different, although the closer he got to his destination, the heavier the air became.

Driving the streets of New York was a little like riding the bumper cars at a carnival. Lanes ceased to exist, and there was no place for common courtesy. It was an adventure in every-man-for-himself, and this morning was no different. Logan found Mike Winters's office and parked in the garage. He checked the collar of his white button-down in the rearview mirror, ran his fingers through his hair, and sank his father's Stetson on his head. He'd look like a buddy in out of town having a chat with Mike. *Not a threat. Not a threat at all.*

The elevator was crowded with tired-eyed bankers holding steaming cups of caffeine and dark briefcases, and eyeing a sexy blonde in a red dress. The business world was a curious one to Logan. It seemed to be filled with wannabes. *Wanna-be single, wanna-be rich, wanna-be anywhere else but here.* Logan had never experienced the *wanna-be* scenario, except when he'd received the news of that attack on his parents. *A burglary gone bad,* that's what they'd called it. Fucking police couldn't track down his father's killer. Logan had to do everything himself.

He followed two suits out of the elevator and eyed the brunette behind the large, curved reception desk that read METRO FINANCIAL across the front in big blue letters.

"Hey there, darlin'." The Midwestern twang played out in Logan's voice when he needed it. Though he wasn't from the Midwest, he and his brothers had lived and worked at their parents' friend Hal Braden's ranch in Weston every summer from the time they were kids until they went away to college. His father insisted that working on a ranch for a few weeks each year would build character. Logan had enjoyed the work, and he'd enjoyed the friendships with Hal and his six children even more.

"Hi. Can I help you?" The pretty receptionist's eyes grazed over Logan's chiseled features to his broad chest.

Logan leaned in closer and lowered his voice. "I'm here to see an old buddy of mine, Mike Winters."

She typed something into her computer and fluttered her thick lashes up at him. "And your name is?"

"I'd rather not be announced, if you don't mind." He lowered his voice again and lathered on his best country-boy twang. "We're old college buddies and I'd like to surprise him, if it's all the same to you. Of course, if a beautiful, important woman like yourself wants my name and number, well…" He threw in a wink for good measure.

"I…Um…"

"My, my. You are sexy when you're flustered."

She fluttered her lashes again and pointed to a set of double glass doors off to the right. "You can…um…find Mr. Winters through there, second door on the right."

"Thank you, darlin'." Logan tipped his hat with a nod and went in search of Mr. Winters. The interior offices were set up like a bullpen, with glass-walled offices lining the exterior walls and cubicles filling the remaining space. Logan found Mike Winters's name on a plaque beside the second door. Logan watched Winters through the glass as he took a phone call. His hair was neatly combed, his suit finely pressed. To a stranger he'd look like a clean-cut businessman. Logan had seen the wolf behind the mask, and as he pushed through the glass door and Mike lifted his eyes, Logan counted the seconds until recognition hit. Mike's eyes widened, and the blood drained from his face. He stood from his plush leather seat, taking a step back with the phone at his ear.

"I've…I've got to go. I'll call you back." He fumbled as he set the receiver on the cradle and held his hands up, palms out. He was going to need more than that if this talk didn't go well. "What do you want?"

"Sit down," Logan commanded, all traces of Midwestern hospitality gone.

Mike stood stock-still. Apparently he wanted to do this the hard way.

Logan took two determined steps around the side of his desk, and Mike sank into the chair.

"I'm sorry. I'm—"

"Shut your fucking mouth."

Mike's jaw snapped shut.

"Now…" Logan began in a calm voice with a threatening stare as he sat on the corner of the desk. To anyone looking through the glass wall, he'd appear to be an old friend, just as he'd planned.

"This is how we're going to play this game. I visited your home this morning over on Garden Lane. Saw your sweet little blond wife and two towheaded adorable girls."

Mike's jaw clenched, but his trembling limbs gave away his weakness.

"Unless you want that lovely family of yours to find out all about your cheating, raping ways, you're never going to go near NightCaps, or that waitress, again."

"F…fine."

Logan glanced over his shoulder, then slowly drew his gaze across Mike's desk and picked up the picture of his family. "It would also be a damn shame if you visited any other bar, alley, or otherwise unfit environment for a husband and father of two, and threatened another woman." He ran his finger over the image of Mike's pretty young wife, then slid his suit coat to the side and flashed his gun.

Mike gasped, his eyes trained on the black metal handle.

"I'll be watching you, Winters. I'd hate to have that wife of yours become a widow, but if you can't keep your claws to yourself, I think I'd be doing a disservice to womankind by letting you roam the streets." He set the picture down on the desk and leaned in so close he could smell fear on Mike's breath. "You only get this one warning. The next time, my bullet will do the talking."

Logan rose to his feet and smoothed his suit coat. "Oh, and if you contact the police and say I threatened you? Wifey will get a quick visit from the woman you attacked last night, along with the police. Your life will be over quicker than you can say, *Oops.*'"

He tipped his hat and left Mike to figure out how to leave his office with piss-wet pants.

Chapter Six

STELLA AWOKE FEELING refreshed, less stressed than she'd been in ages, and sore. So damn sore. The kind of achiness in her hips and the back of her thighs that only came from great sex and multiple orgasms. God, it had felt good to be with a man again. To be in Logan's arms, to feel his strength and revel in his touch, to feel him stroking emotions and sensations she'd long ago forgotten. The way he'd claimed her lips with demand and passion—just thinking about being with him made her body hum. She'd been conflicted when he'd left in the wee hours of the morning. She'd felt herself warming to him and wanted to ask him to stay, but she was in no position to wake up in that man's arms. She was a broken woman, on the run from a guy who would get out of jail in a few short days. No, leading Logan on was the last thing either of them needed.

She showered and dressed, then stripped her bed to wash her sheets before she had to leave for work. She had only one pillow, and last night Logan had used it and she'd rested her head in the crook of his arm. She brought the pillowcase to her nose and breathed in his fresh, masculine scent, allowing herself a rare moment of reflection. *That's it, babe. Come for me. Come for us.* The look in his eyes when he'd said it—dark and sensual, with a hint of surprise—had turned her on and confused the hell out of her. She'd felt something between them that was definitely more than a quick hookup. She loved the way he'd taken control and the way he'd checked in with her before taking his mouth to her, before entering her, searching her eyes, making sure they were still on the same page. They were on the same page, all right. They were in the same damn novel.

Logan was nice, and she wasn't used to *nice*.

Ugh. What on earth was she doing? Who had sex with a guy after being attacked by a psycho? Maybe she was really messed up after all. Maybe Kutcher had ruined all the normal things about her that she'd once relied on. She glanced up at the calendar hanging on the wall beside the pantry. Her stomach felt queasy as she lifted the red marker from the counter and x-ed out another day. Three more days until Kutcher was released.

Three more days until her veil of safety would be shredded to pieces. *Survivor* used to be a term that went along with television shows and hot alpha men in thick leather boots and fisherman type vests, or people who had fallen ill to disease and fought their way healthy again. Now *survivor* was a term Stella likened to herself. She was a survivor, and she had every intention of continuing to fit the definition.

She threw her sheets in the washer, then went into the kitchen to get a cup of coffee. Her kitchen was small, with one long counter, a small sink, and two hanging cabinets on either side of a small window. She liked small areas. There weren't many places a person could hide, unlike her old house, where every room was like a burglar's playground. Or rather, Kutcher's playground. She shivered with the memory of stripping down for her shower and catching the closet door opening out of the corner of her eye. She'd been lucky he'd only stabbed her twice before a neighbor came over because he'd heard her screaming. Kutcher had escaped out the back, and the next afternoon,

Stella had escaped Mystic for good.

It had taken her a solid six weeks to heal. She pushed the painful memories away, and her mind drifted to Heath. He'd been so kind to her, so gentle and professional when he was examining her. She thought about the questions he'd asked when he'd seen the scars. *How did you get these scars? They look fairly recent.* And her ridiculous answers. *Car accident, a few months ago.* She'd been shocked when he didn't press her for more information, and now she wondered if he'd mentioned the scars to Logan.

She couldn't worry about that. Not now. She had bigger things on her mind. With a deep inhalation, she focused on cleaning up the apartment.

An hour later, with the bed freshly made and a to-go cup in hand, Stella walked out of her apartment and locked the door behind her.

"Good morning, Stormy," Mrs. Fairly called from the balcony above Stella's door. She was a stout, kind woman in her late sixties who always greeted Stella with a smile. After spending so much time avoiding friendships, Stella found Mrs. Fairly to be a bright light in her otherwise lonely days.

"Good morning. It looks like another beautiful day." Stella hoped she hadn't heard her and Logan last night. She'd hated lying to her about her name, and she didn't want to keep piling lies on top of that one, but if she asked about Logan, Stella would have to make something up. Having hot, loud sex was one thing, but admitting it to her sweet landlord was another.

"Yes, it does, and it looks like your handsome gentleman suitor is back." She gazed over the railing of the balcony and pointed toward the street.

The hair on the back of Stella's neck rose. Her mind raced

back to the calendar. She had three more days! Ice ran through her veins as she turned, looking past the crooked metal fencing to the black car parked out by the curb.

No, no, no. Please God. I have three more days. She whipped around and looked up at Mrs. Fairly, her heart shattering in her chest. If Kutcher saw Mrs. Fairly, he could hurt her, too.

"Mrs. Fairly, you should go inside." Fear strangled her words, and she wondered if Mrs. Fairly could hear her.

She heard footsteps behind her. She was not going down without a fight. No fucking way had she survived this long only to be killed in front of her sweet landlord in this rundown neighborhood. With trembling hands, she gripped her keys in her palm, the longest sticking out between her knuckles. It wasn't much, but it was all she had. She clenched her eyes shut and spun around as she swung her arm back, ready to strike, and prayed that her brain wouldn't go blank the way it had behind the bar.

"Whoa!"

A strong hand gripped her wrist as her knee came up and clipped him in the groin. Her eyes flew open as Logan doubled over in pain.

"Oh no. Logan!"

"Stormy? Why?" Mrs. Fairly peered down at her in horror.

"I'm sorry. I thought you were someone else. Oh God. I'm sorry." Fear made her shake as she apologized to Logan repeatedly and tried to reassure Mrs. Fairly.

"He's teaching me self-defense. It's all in fun," she said to Mrs. Fairly, hoping she'd buy the explanation.

Logan grimaced as he waved to Mrs. Fairly.

Mrs. Fairly shook her head. "You kids have strange ways of having fun."

After Mrs. Fairly went inside, Logan turned pained eyes toward Stormy. "Why didn't you do that to the attacker last night?"

"I don't...I..." Tears stung her eyes as she tried to pull herself together.

The muscle in Logan's jaw bunched. He drew her into his strong arms and held her tight.

"It's okay. You did good," he assured her through his obvious discomfort.

"Good? I probably broke something *down there*."

"Well, there is *one* way to find out."

She couldn't help but smile at the tease. "What are you doing here? I thought you were Kutcher." She cringed. She didn't mean to say his name, and by the way Logan's hand had stilled on her back, she knew he didn't miss a beat.

Still a little shaky, she pushed from his arms and tried to distract him from what she'd said. "Why are you here? You scared the crap out of me."

"I came to take you to work." The pain in his eyes receded, giving way to the seductive pools of blue she'd fallen into last night.

She looked at his white button-down and cleanly pressed jeans. The cowboy boots he wore were curious, after his polished businessman image of the night before. *Come for us.* Her body heated with the memory. She couldn't do this, couldn't bring him into the nightmare that was her life.

"I can walk."

"Stormy." He followed her out front. "All right, then I'll walk you to work. I want to talk to you."

"We *talked* last night." What was with him? Why was he zeroing in on her?

He moved closer, placed a hand on her back. "We did more than talk, darlin'. That's not what I had in mind for the way to work, but now that you bring it up…"

"*Tsk*." She bit the insides of her cheeks to keep from laughing and stopped short of the corner, planting her hands on her hips and staring at too-damn-handsome-for-his-own-good Logan. He really was beautiful. Her mother would call him a real *panty-dropper*. She'd be right about that. He hadn't shaved, and the thick stubble that had abraded her thighs in the most delicious way last night had grown even thicker. She unleashed the insides of her cheeks and let her smile roll with the memory.

"What?" He cocked a brow, and she could tell he was enjoying teasing her just as much as she was enjoying being teased. When you're hiding from the world, teasing didn't come around often, and when it did, it was usually met with fear. His teasing was met with a fluttering in her stomach that she was trying hard to ignore.

"That was a onetime thing." She was pleased that she sounded serious even though she didn't feel it.

"Uh-huh." He guided her across the street.

"What's with the cowboy boots?" Did he really intend to walk her to work like a sixth grader carrying her books?

"Going back to my mama's roots." Mischief filled his baby blues.

When they reached the main road, the sidewalks were crowded. Stella scanned the crowd, looking for Kutcher. Would she ever be free from his threat? She stole a glance at Logan and realized he was scanning the crowd as closely as she was.

"So your mom is from out West?" His hand felt like it had seared his brand into her skin.

"Colorado. Where are you from?"

"Mysti—" She stopped herself from revealing the town she was from. Unfortunately, the glimmer in his eyes told her she wasn't quick enough. She blew out a frustrated breath as they waited for the next light to change, and lowered her voice.

"Look, Logan, I'm not really a one-night-stand girl, but aren't they supposed to be one night? I don't get why you showed up at my house, or why you're walking me to work. Shouldn't you be out doing important PI stuff?"

They crossed with the crowd. "I *am* doing important PI stuff."

"No, really. Why are you doing this? I'm fine. I've been walking to work since I moved here. I think I can handle it."

"Oh, I know you can." He slid her a serious look. "Stormy." He stopped walking. "Listen, after what we did last night, don't you think you can tell me your real name?"

So that's what this was all about? "Why? Are you keeping a log of the women you've slept with?"

He stepped in close, their bodies grazing from knee to chest. Stella's pulse quickened.

"I'm not keeping a log. I'm trying to keep you safe. That's it. That and the fact that I like you. I feel a connection to you. You can deny it, but I saw it in your beautiful eyes last night."

My beautiful eyes?

He ran his knuckle slowly down her cheek, and she felt her nipples harden at the intimate touch. She fought hard to push the desire to kiss him down deep, tried to avert her eyes so she wouldn't be sucked into his, and was unable to do either. He stepped closer, and she breathed in his fresh, masculine scent. She needed to try even harder to push away the rush of emotions his scent evoked.

"Feel that? That's not one-night-stand heat you're feeling.

Trust me. I've had enough of them to know. One-night stands end after one night. This is lingering, babe, in the best kind of way." He pressed his cheek to hers. "Make no mistake. I want to linger inside of you, all day long."

She couldn't breathe. Couldn't think. Felt herself go damp and her knees weaken, and grabbed ahold of him to keep from dropping to the sidewalk.

"And from your grip on my arm, you want to wrap those pretty long legs of yours around me. *Me*, Stormy. Not some other random guy."

He pressed his lips to her cheek and guided her forward. She had no idea how her legs were carrying her. People pushed past in a blur of movement while she tried to get her brain to start firing again. He was right. She wanted Logan so badly that just the thought of him brought back memories of him perched above her, his muscles straining against the pleasure, holding back his release until she achieved hers. She could still feel every inch of him moving in and out of her, and if she thought hard enough she could remember the feel of his impressive girth in her mouth, taste the saltiness of his come as it covered her tongue and slid down her throat.

Oh God. What am I doing?

She had no place in her life for a guy like Logan. She cleared her throat and forced herself to focus.

"Logan." *Talk, talk, talk. Come on, Stella. You can say this.*

She didn't want to push him away. She wanted more of him.

His arm moved up and claimed her shoulder as they arrived at NightCaps. It was ten thirty, and for a moment she wondered how he knew when she was expected at work.

"Yes, *Stormy*?" He said *Stormy* with so much sarcasm that

she couldn't suppress a smile.

She needed to change the subject, because as much as she wanted him, she also knew it was selfish to give in and admit whatever was simmering between them felt like way more than a one-night stand. Logan didn't need her life weighing him down.

"How did you know what time I had to be at work?"

"I saw it on the schedule when we were in the office." He slid his free hand casually into his pocket.

"God, you're like the worst kind of stalker." She looked away knowing that wasn't anywhere near the truth. Kutcher was the worst kind of stalker. Logan was a sexy, caring stalker.

He drew her chin back with his index finger.

"No." His intense stare went warm and soft, drawing her in again. "I'm the best kind. I'll keep you safe. Tell me about Kutcher."

"How...?" She remembered how he knew his name. She'd let it slip. She didn't know what his game was. He must want something, or maybe he just wanted to get laid again. She'd cut loose for one night. She wasn't going there again—even if every step made the muscles she hadn't remembered she'd had spike with the most exquisite reminders of their night together.

"Kutcher, Stormy. Where can I find him?"

"Oh no, Logan. You can't do anything. This isn't your problem. I can take care of myself."

His arched brow said everything that was sailing through her mind.

"Let me rephrase that. I can handle it. I've got three days to figure it out." Her heart raced at the realization that Kutcher's time in jail was speeding to an end.

His eyes narrowed. "Three days to figure what out? Stormy,

if some guy is looking for you, New York isn't that big. If he's good, he'll find you."

"He's better than good," she said in a hushed tone, hating to admit that Kutcher was good at anything. The bastard.

Logan stepped in closer and lifted her chin so she was forced to look at him. His eyes warmed again, the way they had last night. When he spoke, his tone was sweet, caring, and it tugged at all the places that made her want to go soft in his arms.

"Stormy, no one's better at tracking than me. Let me keep you safe. Give me something to go on. Why three days? Why the timeline? Is he out of the country? In jail?"

Why did he have to make her feel so vulnerable? She needed to be strong, and with him she felt like strong wasn't strong enough, like she needed *him*. After last night's attack, she wasn't so sure she didn't.

"He's found me everywhere I've ever gone. I barely escaped with my life, Logan. I...I'm afraid to tell you who I am, because I'm afraid he'll make the connection somehow and then he'll come after you."

The muscles in his jaw tightened. "I felt the scar on the back of your left shoulder and the other just beside your spine."

Stella's blood ran cold. She turned out of his reach, breathing hard, feeling the pain of the knife as if it were entering her skin for the first time. Kutcher had gotten her bad that time. She should have turned him in, shouldn't have lied about her attacker, but she'd been too scared that he'd avoid the police and come back and finish the job.

Logan's arms snaked around her waist, his cheek met hers again, and she closed her eyes, willing her tears away.

"You're not alone in this. Let me help. Just tell me this, is he a free man?"

She shook her head.

"Good. That's good. Then I have three days to make sure he stays in the pen."

She was trembling, and she didn't know if it was from the memories, the threat of Kutcher's release, or the strength of Logan's grip. His heat seeped into her skin through her thin cotton shirt, and she imagined his strength finding its way in, too. She held on to that thought as she reached for the door. Logan got to it first and held it closed.

"I've got to get to work." She hated herself for sounding so ungrateful, but she was scared, and she liked Logan more than she probably should, which she knew could put him in danger. And he was as relentless as Kutcher, only in a good way. She had no clue how to handle the emotions swirling within her. Should she throw herself into Logan's arms and accept the help he was willing to provide and give in to the feelings that were developing at the speed of light, or run as fast and as far away as she could get before Kutcher came after her?

He slid a cell phone into her pocket. "That has my number in it. Promise me you'll use it if anyone bothers you today, or if you're scared, or if you get a bad feeling and need someone who'll understand that you're not just freaking out."

"You bought me a phone?"

"I have several. That one can't be tracked. Now give me yours. Let's see how this guy is tracking you down."

She rolled her eyes. "What does that mean?"

"It means that I can read you like a book and I'm tired of asking nicely. You're on the run from a guy who's getting out of jail in a few days. You're scared shitless that he'll find you in this hellhole of a city. That tells me that he's found you before, maybe more than once. You're not a stupid woman, so he found you when you were running. Am I right?"

"What? How can you…?"

He arched a brow again. The look suited him. It was snarky, and coupled with the ticking up of the right side of his mouth, it softened his serious edge. Knowing he wasn't going to let it go, she dug into her purse and handed him the phone.

He scrolled through her settings. "You don't use a password?"

She shrugged. "Why? Who's going to look at my phone?"

"Where did you get your phone?" He took out the SIM card and the battery.

"My phone? Kutcher gave me the phone, but it's my plan, so it's not like he can track me with a find my phone app or anything. Besides, he's in jail, so…"

He shook his head. "This is just one way he's probably tracking you. People smuggle cell phones into jails all the time."

She felt like she'd been punched in the stomach. How could she have been so stupid? "You mean…all this time I thought he had people tracking me, it was that stupid phone?" She fisted her hands and groaned.

"It's okay. You didn't know. Let's focus on what we need to do. What else do you carry with you that you've had since you left Mystic?"

"What do you mean? Like my purse? My clothes? I feel like such an idiot."

"Stormy, you're not an idiot. You're just not a drug-running bastard who knows all the tricks. Think of things you don't wash. Suitcase? Wallet? I saw a picture next to your bed. Did you bring that from home or have it made since you left?"

Stella thought of the implications of what he was saying, and the pieces began to fall into place.

"You think he bugged my stuff?" She felt like she'd swallowed a brick. Why hadn't she thought of that? "Oh God."

She handed him her purse. "I took this and everything in it. My backpacks are in my closet."

"I saw them. The photo beside your bed?"

"My mom." The idea of Kutcher tracking her through a picture of the woman she loved most in the world made her feel sick. "I brought it."

"I need two things, and you're not going to like either."

He sounded like her mother's oncologist the day he told her and her mother that her mother had cancer. She clutched his arm, needing his strength once again.

"I need your permission to go into your apartment and check out those things, and I need your permission to take your picture."

"Yes, you can go into my apartment. My keys are in my purse—but take my picture?"

He gave a single curt nod with a stone face.

If he was right about Kutcher, then she owed him a hell of a lot more than a picture.

"Fine. Why?"

He took out his cell phone before she could change her mind and snapped a picture. "Because if you won't tell me who you are, I need to figure it out myself."

"Is there anything you *can't* figure out?"

"Let's hope not." His brows knitted together. "Stormy, if there's anything else you can tell me that might help keep him in jail, please tell me."

"He was a big coke dealer, but I don't know much about how he did it except that he had other guys working for him and he sold to really wealthy clients." Revealing the secret that had nearly gotten her killed made her feel lighter, like she'd been carrying around a bowling ball on her chest for the past few months and she could finally take a deep breath.

He cupped her cheek. "Thank you for trusting me."

She did trust him. Completely. And as good as that felt, it also scared her, because even though she knew he wasn't anything like Kutcher, once upon a time she'd trusted Kutcher, too.

He pulled the door open. "Shall we?"

"What are you going to do, sit and babysit me all day?"

"No." He waved to Dylan behind the bar.

Dylan smiled. "Logan." He shook his head, like he should have known Logan would show up with her. "How're you doing, Stormy?"

"Fine." She saw the look of approval Dylan gave Logan.

Was this all a big joke? They'd probably placed bets on whether he'd get laid last night. Dylan hadn't struck her as that type of guy, and unless her judgment was way off base, Logan was anything *but* that kind of guy. If he were just out to get laid, he would have taken off last night and never shown his face again. Instead, he was going to try to help her with Kutcher. Not that she thought anyone could do a damn thing where Kutcher was concerned, but she liked feeling as if she wasn't in this alone.

She went into the office to clock in. She turned and Logan was *right there*.

"Hi, darlin'," he said quietly.

"H-hi. I…um…have to get to work." Why did he have to be so good-looking? So kind? So in control and confident? So damn *big*? She sighed inside, adding *a great lover* to the most ridiculous list of woes she'd ever made. A big, protective, good-looking, great lover who took the time to walk her to work and beat the snot out of some drunk guy who was harassing her. Even now, when she wasn't in imminent danger, she felt safe with him. That was why he was there, wasn't it? The big broody soldier helping the damsel in distress?

God, she hated that idea almost as much as she hated Kutcher for making her feel that way.

"I'll be back to take you home after your shift."

"Logan." She gave him a deadpan stare, sort of hoping it might dissuade him and sort of hoping it wouldn't.

"Stormy." He smiled, and she noticed a scar at the edge of his jaw that she hadn't noticed before.

Without thinking, she reached up and touched the bare spot in his stubble.

"How did you get that?" She remembered the pain she'd seen in his eyes last night when she'd felt like he was opening his soul by sharing his secrets.

He shrugged. "Don't remember." He brought her fingers to his lips and kissed them. "I paid a visit to that guy from last night. He shouldn't bother you anymore."

"You...How? When?" The guy from last night? But Logan was gone only a few hours. How could he possibly have tracked the guy down so fast? And why would he?

He touched her elbow. "The *best* kind of stalker, remember? Only I'm not a stalker at all." He leaned down and kissed her cheek, then turned to leave.

"Where are you going?" She didn't want him to go. Even the few steps away that he'd just taken made her feel vulnerable. She was being stupid. She had handled life before him. Certainly one night of amazing sex and a few sweet gestures couldn't make her into a needy girl.

"To do important PI stuff." He blew her a kiss and disappeared, leaving her feeling like she'd just met the Lone Ranger.

Chapter Seven

IT WASN'T HARD to track down Kutcher. There was only one inmate in Connecticut with that surname, Carl Kutcher. The trickier part was tracking down the people who had been associated with him on the outside. If Logan could prove that Kutcher was still dealing drugs while in jail, it would make keeping him behind bars much easier. It had been Logan's experience that major dealers don't stop dealing because they're in the pen. They just get more creative.

Using his sources, he was able to track down four possible drug connections, two outside Connecticut, two within an hour of Mystic. He jotted down the information on the connections and eyed his vibrating cell phone on the edge of his desk.

Heath.

He'd expected a call, especially after what his mother had said. Heath possessed all the qualities that were common of being the eldest child. He was overprotective of his very capable younger brothers, each of whom had bodies built for a brawl and sharp minds that didn't need babysitting. He'd always gotten superior grades, and of all his siblings, Heath was the one who had gotten in the least amount of trouble over the years. He was prone to being just careful enough never to get caught, whereas Logan, Jackson, and Cooper had always been a little reckless.

He answered the call while scrolling through the information on his computer.

"Hey, bro. Thanks for helping out last night."

"Sure thing. Ma said you came by."

Logan heard voices and shuffling in the background and knew his brother was doing rounds at the hospital.

"Yeah. I was out that way and just checking in." He didn't want to admit that the attack on Stormy had rustled up bad memories and driven him to check on his mother.

"Good. She was glad to see you. I had coffee with her this morning before work." Heath covered the mouthpiece and said something Logan couldn't make out, then came back on the line. "Sorry, man. Listen, I'm just calling to see how *Stormy* is doing. Please tell me you got her real name before you took her home."

Logan was only half paying attention, as he had another hit for a connection to Kutcher, this one on the outskirts of Mystic.

Bingo.

He jotted down the information. "That would be a negative, but I'll get it."

Heath didn't respond.

"What, Heath? Spit it out."

"Just...you know, Logan. It's been a long time since I've seen you look at someone like you were looking at her. Possessively."

"She was hurt. I had just nailed her attacker." He'd deny whatever he was feeling to his brothers until he understood it himself. Hell, he didn't even know why he was telling Stormy that he felt so much for her after one night. It wasn't like him to latch on to anyone. He'd never had a serious girlfriend, and he sure as hell wasn't looking for one.

"Listen, she's obviously got some shit going on. I'm just trying to find out what it is. It *is* my job, you know."

"Yeah, okay." He could tell by Heath's voice that he wasn't buying it. "Well, dinner at Mom's Sunday night. You're on for the wine."

"I'll be there." Logan would never miss another dinner with their mother.

After they ended the call, Logan called his buddy Marco.

"Yo." Marco Ortega was a mean son of a bitch with long black hair, tattoos on every inch of flesh save for his face and neck, and the kind of voice that made a man's blood run cold. Marco had been in and out of jail for most of his twenties, which afforded him firsthand knowledge about the underworld of what goes on behind bars. He was one of those guys who were on the right side of the wrong side of the law, doing things that skirted the legal line, but always for good purpose.

"It's me. I need a favor." Logan filled Marco in on Mike Winters and hired him to tail Winters for the next four weeks. "I want to know everywhere he goes. Leave out no details. I wanna know when this guy takes a shit, got it?"

"Got it, boss." Marco was loyal to Logan for many reasons, the least of which was that Logan had cleared his brother of a felony by tracking down the real perp when no one else had given a damn. "And if he goes near the bar or the girl?"

"Detain him until I can get there."

His next call was to Dylan at the bar. Logan didn't expect Dylan to spill his guts. Like the rest of the Wilds and Bads, he was one loyal son of a bitch, and by his reaction to Stormy last night, Logan assumed that stretched to her now as well.

"What took you so long?" Dylan knew him well.

"Had a few things to take care of. You working all day?"

"Yup. Don't worry. I'll keep my eyes open."

"You know anything about her past?" Logan trusted Dylan to give him enough to go on, even if he didn't want to breach Stormy's confidence.

"Probably less than you know after the time you spent with her."

He heard the smile in Dylan's voice.

"One thing, Logan. I pay her in cash, and she mails half her earnings to someone back in Mystic."

"How do you know?"

"I saw her doing it once and asked about it. She said she had a sick relative. That's all I know."

"Dyl, why'd you hire her?" The minute the words were out, he knew the answer and regretted asking.

"You know why." Dylan's family had had their own crisis long before Logan's family had had theirs. Dylan had a younger sister who'd died when they were kids, and he had a soft spot for keeping women safe. "Logan, are you just messing with her? Because she's been hurt enough."

"Have you ever seen me walk a woman to work?" Logan shifted in his seat, still uncomfortable with the way his stomach got funky when he thought of Stormy.

Dylan laughed. "Didn't want to call you on that."

"Yeah, well, neither do I. Thanks for watching out for her, man. I gotta run."

A few more phone calls and a little computer hacking allowed Logan to track the IP for the recipient of the SIM-card information collected from Stormy's phone. Thank God Kutcher was a cheapskate and used shabby products. He'd made it child's play for Logan to get the information he needed. After shutting down the ability of the tracker and making more phone calls, Logan arranged for Kutcher's cell to be tossed.

With most of the annoying aspects of his morning taken care of, Logan scrolled to the picture of Stormy he'd taken outside of NightCaps. His stomach clenched at the palpable fear in her green eyes. They were eyes that had seen too much, and last night, when he'd seen her let go, a hint of the fear had remained. He wanted to wash that fear away, every last evil speck of it. Logan had seen people's looks change once a threat was removed, and Stormy was already beautiful. He could only imagine how she'd look once he nailed that Kutcher bastard to the wall.

He uploaded the picture to Google Images and found four hits immediately. Her high school graduation photo. She was thicker then, curvier, and hell if her catlike eyes weren't carefree and clear. Logan held on to that image as he wrote down her real name—*Stella Krane*—and the name of the high school she'd attended. Before now he'd have put the name Stella together with an older woman, stern and spindly. Funny how a face could change the connotation of a name, but in his mind, Stella Krane and Stormy were one sensual, strong woman.

"What is it about you, Stormy Krane?" He still couldn't think of her as Stella. Not after having to dig up the information. When he'd earned her trust enough for *her* to tell him her real name, then and only then would he call her Stella.

He checked out a few of the other photos. Several were posted on the Facebook profile pages of girls who had gone to the same high school Stella had attended. She was smiling in all of them. What he wouldn't give to see her smile like that. He surfed the Facebook images for a while and found one linked to a *Mystic Messenger* newspaper article about Stella's mother, Judy Krane. It was an announcement for a fundraiser to help with

Judy's medical bills. Cancer. *Fucking cancer.* No wonder she sent money home. He pushed back from the computer and pinched the bridge of his nose, thinking of the little sister Dylan had lost. Life was full of ass kickers. Logan was going to make damn sure that Stormy got back to her mother, even if he had to take Kutcher out himself.

An hour later Logan stood in Stormy's kitchen feeling as though he were peering into her private life where he shouldn't be. If she were a client and he needed to gather clues, this might be typical. But Logan didn't sleep with clients, and Stormy wasn't a client. He forced himself not to think of her as the woman who was stirring up all sorts of emotions in him and did his best to put his feelings aside and turn on his private-investigator instincts.

Logan was methodical in his search efforts. He walked down to the bedroom, planning to work his way back out to the front door. In the light of day the bedroom appeared very much like Stormy, efficient with an underlying womanly charm. He was sure the apartment came furnished, and he was equally as confident that Mrs. Fairly wouldn't have asked for a social security number or proof of identification. She'd probably taken Stormy at face value.

Being in her bedroom brought memories of the night before rushing back. The muscles on the back of his neck tightened as he was reminded of discovering the rough edges of the scar on the back of her shoulder. When he'd felt the other scar beside her spine, his blood had gone cold, stirring all of the protective urges he usually reserved for family. Those urges had only become stronger in the hours since.

He'd get this asshole if it was the last thing he did.

In the closet he thoroughly checked each hanger, seeking a

stick-on tracker or a chip adhered to the plastic. He searched every seam and pocket of the few pieces of clothing she had in her closet, then moved to the backpack and other things on the shelf above. Once he was satisfied that there were no tracking devices in the closet, he searched her bedroom, inspecting the lower drawers of her dresser first, but avoiding the top drawer women usually reserved for lingerie. He searched her perfectly folded jeans and tops. The Wesleyan T-shirt was telling. People who were on the run generally took the items with them that meant something. He'd already discovered that she was a Wesleyan graduate, and the shirt told him that she was proud of that accomplishment. He'd seen Stormy's harsh exterior slip several times, and he wondered how much she'd had to change since running from Kutcher.

Forcing his personal interest in Stormy away again, he searched through her top drawer. Sifting through her bras and panties sent his mind right back to being inside her, ravishing her delicious mouth, seeing her lips wrapped around his cock.

Fuck. Now he was hard.

Logan closed his eyes and counted backward from fifty. At five he was still at half-mast. There was no ridding his mind of her.

He gritted his teeth and forced himself to at least *think* like the PI that he was. He reached into the drawer and assessed her lingerie. Matching lace bras and panties, although not high-end, were not department-store brands either. Another bit of intel for his Stormy file. At some point, she probably had a pretty good life.

The more he tried to disengage his personal feelings, the more difficult it became. Standing just a foot away from where he'd been when she'd taken his cock in her mouth and swallowed everything he'd had to give made it nearly impossible. His cock stirred just thinking of their slick bodies moving together as he held her knees at his sides and she met each powerful thrust with a lift and tilt of her hips.

Great. He was hard again.

He ran a frustrated hand through his hair and slid his eyes from the bed to the framed picture of her mother. The hair on the back of his neck stood up, and his erection softened. He took out the photo and found a tracking device attached to the inside of the frame. He tore the fucker out. He knew exactly what it was, because he'd used them a dozen times. This one was a cheap piece of shit, like the traceable SIM card Kutcher had put in Stormy's phone. A knockoff brand that sent data through the Internet. The guy knew what he was doing. He'd probably used them in his drug business.

He pocketed the device, then carefully put the picture back into the frame and set it beside the bed. He picked up the pillow and brought it to his nose. *Freshly washed.* He had a feeling that the harshness Stormy portrayed wasn't the only change she'd made either for Kutcher or while running from him. He'd had the distinct feeling when they were together that she was acting how she thought she should rather than how she might if she weren't trying to escape her fear for a few hours. He was all for rough and dirty sex, but Stormy wasn't the type of woman you fucked hard and walked away from. She was the type of woman you made love to, while reserving the hard fucking for the intimate, wild, sexy nights couples shared. But day-to-day? She seemed more the flowers and wine type of girl, and the more he looked around her apartment, the more pieces of her life he put together, and the more he wanted to know about her.

Logan methodically checked every item in the bathroom and the laundry closet, then worked his way through the pantry and the kitchen cabinets. He eyed the calendar on the wall and flipped back through the pages. She'd marked off the date Kutcher had been put in jail, and had been counting down the days until his release, marking each one with a red *X*. He couldn't imagine the fear she carried with her every moment of the day. He flipped back through the months, finding angry black marks every few weeks. It didn't take a genius to figure out that those were the dates Kutcher had taken his hands to her.

Son of a bitch.

There was no way in hell he was going to feed Stormy to that wolf. He went back into the bedroom and packed her bags, careful to take everything, from her mother's picture to her toothbrush. Then he went through the motions of checking all the places he thought Stormy might hide cash or other valuables she wouldn't want someone to steal. He checked under the mattress, in the ceiling tiles, above the cabinets, under the sink. He looked beneath the table to see if she'd taped anything there. Nothing. He looked around the room, trying to climb into Stormy's head. The trouble was, he didn't think Stormy was in her own head lately. She was in the head of the woman she'd become, and he had no idea how to discern the difference from this standpoint. He eyed a ceramic cookie jar on the counter and on a whim lifted the head of the ceramic cat and reached inside.

Bingo.

A thick envelope full of cash.

Christ, Stormy. He made a mental note to teach her about safer hiding places for her valuables.

His heart did that funky thing it had been doing since he'd met her. He ignored it, aware of the time ticking by, and stuffed the envelope in his back pocket. He brought the bags out to his car and went to pay a visit to Mrs. Fairly.

She answered the door wearing a light blue housecoat. She looked older than Logan's mother, with gray hair and a friendly, round face. Recognition spiked in her eyes, and she smiled warmly.

"Hello there."

"Hi, Mrs. Fairly. I'm Logan Wild." He held out a hand and was met with a limp handshake.

"Yes. You're Stormy's friend."

"That's right. She asked me to come by to get her things. We're going on a trip, and I wanted to settle up her remaining lease."

"Oh, my. Is she leaving for good?" A crease formed between her brows.

"Yes, I believe so. How much rent are you due?" He thought of his mother, and the idea of her needing to take in a stranger for money bothered him. Mrs. Fairly had opened her house to Stormy, and even though he'd just met them both, he was thankful that Stormy had found a safe place to live.

"She's on a month-to-month, dear. She's paid up for this month."

His soft heart got the better of him. "And how much was she paying per month?"

"Nine hundred dollars, but she's all paid up, as I said."

After giving her a check for six months' rent, Logan gave her a talk about not opening the door for strangers and then he headed back to his office. It was too late to drive to Mystic if he wanted to pick up Stormy after her shift, and at least for now he knew she was safe. She may not like it, but until he could ensure that Kutcher would never bother her again, she was stuck with him.

Chapter Eight

THE DAY DRAGGED by despite the continuous flow of customers. Stella could hardly believe that the man who looked cold and possibly dangerous the first night she'd seen him at the bar made her feel safe and like she wasn't alone for the first time since this nightmare began. She tried to ignore the other desires he was sparking.

She looked up at the door for the hundredth time today. Each time she did, a chill ran across her shoulders. She wasn't sure if it was from wanting to see Logan or out of fear that Kutcher would walk through the door and drag her God knew where. Although that wasn't Kutcher's style. He was stealthy, like a ninja. He'd be more likely to hide in her apartment or in an alley so he could drag her into the darkness and leave her body in a Dumpster.

"He'll be here," Dylan said. "You still have fifteen minutes until you're off work, and Logan, he never drops the ball."

She tried to smile, but her head was still wrapped around thoughts of Kutcher. He'd been abusive, but she knew that wasn't the reason he'd wanted her dead. She'd made a mistake the last time he'd come after her. As he was pressing the sharp point of the knife to her skin, she'd said, *I won't tell them about the ring.*

The ring. That's what he'd called his drug-dealing business.

She'd overheard him talking about it and put the pieces of his shady life together. His eyes had glazed over, cold and dark, and as the knife violently tore through her skin, she'd thought her next breath would be her last. The second stab sent her to her knees—and then her neighbor had responded to her screams.

The flow of customers slowed, and Dylan leaned his hip against the bar, kicked one ankle over the other, and crossed his arms. "Do you want to talk?"

Stella leaned against the bar beside him. She'd been hoping he'd ask. She'd shared some of the details about her past with Dylan, like the fact that she was hiding from an abusive ex-boyfriend, although she hadn't told him everything.

"Did you tell Logan about me?"

He shook his head, his dark eyes trained on hers. "I didn't have to. He'd never ask me to breach a confidence. That's not how he rolls. Anything Logan wants or needs to know, he'll find out."

"I got that impression." Her pulse kicked up when the front door opened.

They both looked over at a couple as they walked in and took a seat at a booth. She pushed from the bar to go take their order, and Dylan gently touched her arm.

"Three days left?" Dylan's voice was low and deep, as serious as the day was long.

"Two and a half." The pit of her stomach twisted into a knot.

"Listen to Logan, okay? I don't want to hear about you on the morning news."

She'd listen to Logan. She had no choice. He didn't seem as though he'd give her one. And she wasn't sure she wanted him to.

During the day, the bartenders took on the double duty of handling the floor and the bar. Stella didn't mind. She was glad for the distraction from her thoughts. She took the customers' orders and saw to two other tables before returning to the bar.

The front door opened again. The late-afternoon sun silhouetted Logan's tall, broad frame, every muscle of his chest outlined by a tight black T-shirt. How had she missed the barbed-wire tattoo circling his right bicep? Jeans clung deliciously to his massive thighs, and the bulge to the right of his zipper made her mouth go dry. She knew what magic that impressive bulge could perform.

The door closed behind him, and his face came into focus. The stern set of his jaw and piercing stare told her that he had bad news, but it was the way he closed the distance between them, took her by the arm, and walked with his body practically swallowing her whole that had her pulse working double-time.

LOGAN HAD SPENT the last hour watching the bar from the café across the street. He knew Stormy would be nervous if he sat inside the bar and waited, but he needed to have his eyes on her. As long as she was behind the bar or by the booths against the far wall, he'd been able to see her through the windows. Now her shift was over, and all he could think about was getting her out of there. When they'd tossed Kutcher's cell, they'd found two phones. The fucker had been tracking her all along. Logan had to get her to a safe place. Kutcher had too many friends on the outside to wait out the three days playing cat and mouse, knowing one of Kutcher's cronies could abduct her at any moment. Stormy was a sitting duck.

"You're hurting me," she said in a harsh whisper.

He loosened his grip. He had to find a way to separate the anger that had been mounting since he'd first learned that Kutcher had bought her the phone from his need to protect her. There was no fighting the protective urges he felt toward Stormy, but one thing was for sure: They were done with the physical side of their relationship. He couldn't afford to fuck this up. He needed all of his senses on high alert when he was with her, and if he didn't push aside his feelings for her, he'd never be able to keep his focus where it belonged.

"I'm sorry, sweetheart. We need to talk."

Dylan was talking with another employee by the bar. He lifted his chin in Logan's direction as they passed. Logan had texted him and filled him in on what was going down. He agreed to give Stormy whatever time off she needed, of course, and would have a job waiting for her when the situation was under control.

In the back office, Stormy rubbed her arm, eyeing him from beneath her long dark hair, which had fallen over one eye.

"Just tell me." She lifted her chin and crossed her arms. "I can handle whatever it is."

The underlying hint of desperation in her voice drew him closer. "We have to get out of here. Out of the area. He's been tracking you this whole time. It's not safe."

Her lower lip began to tremble, and her brows knitted together. Logan fought the urge to fold her into his arms and hold her until her fear subsided. He tried to ignore the memory of her mouth on his and the desire to kiss her until neither of them could think about what lay ahead. She couldn't bury this fear in sex, and he couldn't allow himself to be weakened by the thought of it. He drew his shoulders back, steeling himself against his emotions, feeling his body go as cold as it had during every mission he'd ever served. After killing the man who had murdered his father and blinded his mother, he'd worked hard to try to find his way back to some semblance of normal emotions, and he realized now, as he tried to slide into the icy state, that it wasn't until Stormy that the urge to care about anyone other than family had broken through that ice around his heart.

Stormy looked at him with her big, trusting eyes and reached for him. Instinct took over, and he gathered her in his arms, feeling nothing like the soldier he'd been. A soldier wouldn't cave under pressure—a soldier had to protect his heart. Logan was more interested in protecting hers.

He kissed the top of her head as he pressed one hand to her upper back, the other to her lower, and whispered, "I've got you. I won't let anything happen to you."

His blood refused to turn to ice; his heart refused to slip into the frozen state in which it had once spent every waking moment. How the hell was he going to navigate this new terrain? He couldn't let her out of his sight, but if there was any hope in hell of keeping Kutcher behind bars, he had to get to Mystic, and there was no way he was taking her anywhere near there until he was sure the threat of Kutcher was gone.

She fisted her hands in his shirt. "Where will I go? I need to pack."

"I've got all your stuff. We're leaving."

"Where are we going?"

"Let me take care of it." He reached into his back pocket and handed her the envelope he'd found in the cookie jar.

"I...I usually carry that in my purse, but after what happened the other night, I realized my purse could probably get stolen more easily than my apartment could be broken into. Logan, what did you find in my stuff?"

Last night she'd been attacked. This morning, outside her apartment, she'd thought he was Kutcher. He knew from her calendar how long she'd been living in fear of this man, and he wasn't going to give Kutcher another second of power over her. He tucked her under his arm, feeling some of the tension bleed from her shoulders.

"Let's go."

"Please tell me where we're going."

"The only place I know you'll be safe. My cabin."

Chapter Nine

STORMY WAS QUIET on the drive out of the city. She was still fidgeting with the seam of her jeans and hugging the passenger door. They'd stopped at a market before leaving the city, and Logan had stocked up on enough groceries to tide them over for a few days and had picked up sandwiches for dinner, which they'd eaten on the way. He'd hoped she'd close her eyes and get some rest on the drive out to his cabin in the Silver Mountains in Sweetwater, New York, but he'd had no such luck. Every time he stole a glance at her, the thin layer of ice he'd held tenuously in place around his heart since they'd set out for the cabin melted a little more. It was all Logan could do not to pull her against him and help ease her worry. He told her about the tracking devices he'd found and tried to reassure her that he had a plan, although his plan was loosely threaded at the moment, overshadowed by the need to get her to safety. He had less than seventy-two hours to get to Kutcher, and come hell or high water, he'd nail the bastard.

It was dark by the time they wove up the mountain road, led by streaks of moonlight carving paths through the trees. Stormy made a sad noise in her throat that tugged at Logan, wiping away the last of his resolve. He reached for her hand, and for a split second their eyes connected before he had to turn back to the road. In that instant he saw deep wells of sorrow. He wished he were driving his father's old truck, which he kept at the cabin, instead of his car. It had a bench seat, and he could have held her close while he drove.

He turned down the dirt driveway and stopped the car in front of the iron gate. *The hell with professional distance.* Distance was the last thing she needed. She'd had distance for as long as she'd been running. He unhooked his seat belt and hauled his thick body over the console to pull her against him. Her body was rigid at first as he stroked her back. "I've got you. You're safe with me."

Darkness peered through the windows, keeping the sounds of night at bay and leaving them in a bubble of silence. He could have held her all night right there on the secluded drive on the Silver Mountains, but he wanted her safe *and* comfortable. He touched his forehead to hers.

"Hey."

She lifted a tenuous gaze.

"I've got you." He pressed a kiss to her forehead.

For the first time, she looked fragile. Her eyes were soft, her shoulders low. Her walls were coming down, and that made Logan's protective impulses even stronger. He'd been on high alert as they'd left the city and had taken the long way to the property to avoid being tailed. There hadn't been a single set of taillights for the last twenty miles.

He settled back into his seat and used the remote to open the gate, still holding her hand. She leaned her head back and closed her eyes as he drove up the long dark driveway toward the cabin.

Logan parked the car and flicked a code on the remote. Porch and floodlights illuminated a thirty-foot area around the two-bedroom cabin.

"Where are we?"

"Silver Rock Mountains, upstate New York. I own two hundred acres. You'll be safe here. I've got surveillance cameras throughout the property, but there's no need to worry," he assured her. "No one knows you're here."

"Wow. You're like one of those guys in the movies, where in a few hours you can become invisible." She sighed as she unhooked her seat belt. "What I wouldn't give for that skill."

Logan got out of the car and opened her door.

"*And* you're a gentleman." She smiled up at him, looking markedly less worried than she'd been moments before. Logan knew she was good at slipping in and out of the armor she wore in public, and he wasn't buying the no-fear mask she was wearing.

"I guess my mama raised her boys right." He reached for her hand and helped her from the car, then retrieved her bags. He had everything he needed at the cabin, from clothing to tactical gear and equipment.

Out of habit, he scanned the area as they ascended the steps to the wraparound porch.

"I bet this place is gorgeous in the daylight."

"Night or day, if you ask me." Logan pushed the door open and scanned the interior. It was a simple cabin with a bedroom on either end, a small kitchen to the left, and a wood-burning stove surrounded by stone just beyond. Reclaimed barn wood lined the far wall. Logan watched Stormy take in the leather recliners in the living room and the old leather sofa beside the stove. Her boots resounded on the hardwood floors.

"This is exactly how I pictured you'd live." She ran her hand over the marble countertops in the kitchen. "I love how you've combined old barn wood with higher-end elements, and the stainless-steel stove and fridge are a nice touch."

"Careful. Your interior decorator side is showing."

She smiled. "So important PI stuff included digging up my career?"

"Just a little." He didn't want her to feel too exposed, but he wanted her to know that he wasn't oblivious to who she was, so he turned the conversation from her back to the cabin. "My father had a thing for stone. Probably because he could never afford it." Talking about his father made his muscles cord tight, and he didn't know what possessed him to mention his father to Stormy.

He'd bought the property after he'd returned to civilian life, as a place where he could escape the guilt of not being there when his parents needed him. Finding out that guilt stayed with him like white on rice was a harsh reality he'd still not gotten used to. He'd added the stone at the last minute. His father was the hardest-working man Logan had ever known, though he'd never made much money. Logan had carried one image of his father with him for years. They'd just arrived at Hal Braden's ranch in Weston, Colorado, for him and his brothers to work for a few weeks. Hal was a hulking man at six foot six, with shoulders as wide as a doorframe. His father had walked inside beneath Hal's big arm, the two men looking as close as brothers. Logan's father had turned to him and said, *When you build a home, son, do as Hal did. Use stone and wood. Stone for solidity and stability and wood for compassion and warmth.*

He felt the walls closing in on him with the memory and escaped to the bedroom off to the left, where he shrugged Stormy's bags onto the bed. He'd never brought any women to the cabin before. But it had been the first and only place that had come to mind with Stormy. He decided not to dissect that too closely as he watched her through the open bedroom door. She bent to remove her boots, and he tried not to stare, or let his mind wander too far, but seeing her bent at the waist conjured up all sorts of lewd thoughts. He shifted his eyes away.

She's got a guy after her and you're thinking of fucking her. Real nice, Logan.

"That's better." She carried her boots to the mat by the door and wrinkled her brow. "Why are you looking at me like that?"

Logan shook off his lustful haze and joined her in the living room. She sank into the sofa with a sigh and closed her eyes. He paced, too revved up to sit still.

Stormy patted the sofa beside her. "Sit down. You're making me nervous. I thought you said we were safe here."

"We are." He stopped pacing and crossed his arms. Her eyelids were heavy as she curled her feet up beside her and slid a little lower, resting her head on the cushion.

"Then why do you look like a puma guarding its territory? Your shoulders are tight, and you're probably going to crack your teeth you're clenching them so hard."

He smiled at her observation. What she didn't see were the thoughts racing through his mind. The battle between right and wrong. His emotions had already jumped over the invisible line, and he was doing all he could to get back on the right side of it.

"The sheets on the bed are clean if you want to rest." It had been about a two-hour drive from the city, and after working all day and not getting much sleep the night before, she had to be exhausted.

"Are you kidding? How can I sleep knowing you're out here stalking around?"

"Sorry." He went into his bedroom and grabbed the laptop he kept there, then sat beside her on the couch. At least if his mind and hands were busy, he wouldn't be thinking about touching her.

He pulled his cell from his pocket and turned on the hot spot for the Internet, watching her as he waited for it to connect. Her eyelids became hooded, and her arms wrapped around her middle as if she were cold. Logan set the laptop on the coffee table and covered her with the throw from the bedroom.

She pulled it up beneath her chin with a sleepy smile. "Thank you for everything, Logan."

He smiled, feeling the impact of the realization that he'd do anything for her. He sat stock-still, momentarily blown away by the depth of his feelings for her. She sank farther down into the cushions, startling him out of his stupor.

He settled the laptop on his lap and checked on the emails he'd sent that morning to his contacts at the prison where Kutcher was being held. A while later Stormy's feet nudged their way onto his lap, and he shifted his laptop to accommodate them. Her features had softened the way they had last night. She looked peaceful, as if she felt safe, and that last bit made his chest feel full.

Logan forced himself to concentrate on tracking down Bob Kanets, the dealer he hoped he'd be able to coerce into ratting out Kutcher for drug trafficking. If he was successful, it could keep Kutcher behind bars for at least a few more years. An hour later he had a list of Kutcher's associates along with a trail of gas and other receipts marking his territory. He sent a text to Marco and got the lowdown on Winters, who seemed to have taken his advice to heart, going straight from work to home and staying put for the night. Marco would continue to tail him for a month. One piece of shit out of the way.

Stormy shifted beside him, and he wondered if it would be better if she felt like a stranger, because falling for a woman wasn't in his plans, and as he set his laptop on the coffee table and lifted her into his arms, he knew it was exactly what was happening.

He carried her into her bedroom, pulled the blankets back, and set her down on the sheets. Light from the living room provided just enough illumination for him to see her lips curve in a sweet smile.

He debated undressing her so she'd be more comfortable, but didn't trust himself enough to keep his desires in check. Instead, he pulled the covers up, moved her bags to the floor, and checked the locks on the windows. It felt strange to leave the bedroom when he wanted to climb in beside her and hold her safely against him. Keeping a professional distance sucked.

He left the bedroom door cracked open as fatigue settled into his bones. He checked the lock on the front door one last time before stripping down to his briefs and falling into bed.

STELLA AWOKE WITH a start. She thought she'd heard a noise, but she was so tired that she wasn't sure if she really had or if it was part of the nightmare she'd been having about Kutcher. Her eyes darted around the dark, unfamiliar room. Her heart thundered in her chest, and the only thing she heard was the blood rushing through her ears. She took a few deep breaths, telling herself that it was just a dream.

She'd awoken a while ago feeling bound by her clothes, and she'd stripped down to her underwear, taken off her bra, and dug a T-shirt out of her bag. As her heartbeat calmed, she took stock of the positive things in her life. It was one of the ways she'd gotten through the long nights these past few months, because focusing on all she'd left behind or how scared she was would render her useless.

She was alive. That topped the list of blessings.

She was safe in Logan's cabin. *God, Logan.* He'd looked like he was ready to pounce earlier in the evening—either on anyone who came near her, or on her; she'd had a hard time deciphering his desire from his protective instincts. He was a complex man, but she trusted him, and liked him way too much. Great. Now she was getting hot and bothered by just thinking about him.

Her eyes danced around the room to distract herself. There was a large wooden dresser on the far wall, and dark curtains covered the windows. The whole cabin felt masculine. *Like Logan.* She hated sucking him into her nightmare of a life, but at the same time, she was thankful he'd been there when she'd needed him. She heard a noise outside her window, and she clutched the blanket to her chest, holding her breath while she listened to a scratching noise on the deck. She closed her eyes, and when she opened them, she caught sight of a man filling the doorframe with a gun hanging from his right hand, and screamed.

"It's me." Logan pulled her against him as she fought to climb off the other side of the bed. "It's Logan. You're safe."

"I heard a noise," she panted out.

"Raccoons. They wandered onto the deck."

Raccoons. Not Kutcher.

Her heart felt like it was going to explode. She clutched Logan's arms.

"It's okay. No one knows you're here. You're safe. I promise."

"Then why do you have a gun?" she whispered, too afraid to speak louder.

"Habit."

As her mind came into focus, she became aware of his bare chest against her cheek, his thick, bare thighs beneath her. In her panic she must have scrambled onto his lap. She closed her eyes as her fear spun itself into lust. She pulled from his arms but immediately felt vulnerable again.

"St-stay," she pleaded.

He didn't respond immediately, and as her senses righted themselves, she felt the reason he was holding back. As she'd been assessing her own desires, he'd gone gloriously, impressively hard as steel beneath her.

"Not a good idea." His voice was thrillingly low and rough. "I need to be alert."

"Well, I think you've achieved that."

He looked at her out of the corner of his eye, his jaw twitching.

"I just don't want to be alone. Please? We won't..."

She knew they'd both be testing their willpower, and she watched as he fought some kind of silent battle that had his eyes narrowing and his jaw clenching again. He set her off his lap and scrubbed a hand down his face.

"I promise not to touch you." She tried to sound confident, but all of her girlie parts were begging her to lie.

He made a noise deep in his throat that could be read as anger or desire, and the way his muscles were strung tight made her not want to take a chance at guessing the wrong one. He looked away, and when he met her gaze again, his eyes had gone dark and seductive.

"Stormy." He was breathing hard. "It's not *your* touch I'm afraid of."

She thought about that for a minute before it clicked. "*Oh.* Then I won't let you touch me."

He scrubbed his face again.

"Please?" She didn't want to be alone. She hadn't slept in days, and she desperately needed to rest. At least that's what she told herself as she tried not to admit—even to herself—that she wanted to be close to Logan. On the drive up from the city, the distance between them had felt too vast. When they'd arrived at the cabin, she'd wanted to curl up on his lap and feel his arms around her as she rested her head on his shoulder. She was good at lying to herself, but they were momentary lies, chased by a truth she couldn't avoid. She was falling for Logan Wild.

Without a word he set the gun on the bedside table and crawled between the sheets. He lay on his back, the sheet tented by his erection. She pretended not to notice and fought the urge to wrap her body around him like a second skin. He draped his arm over his eyes and lay rigid beside her. She turned onto her side with her back facing Logan, knowing she'd made a mistake. There was no way she'd be able to resist him.

She did feel safe. Safer than she'd ever felt in her life—at least from outside forces. But her heart wasn't safe at all. Logan didn't have anything to gain by helping her. She hadn't offered him money or her body or *anything* in return, and here he was, opening his cabin to her and putting his own life on hold. She inched toward him out of a desire to be close to the man, not the PI, and she felt him tense up even more. Her back met his side. Her legs touched his. His skin was blazing hot, and that heat spread through her like wildfire. She needed to feel his arms around her. Even if they didn't have sex, she wanted to feel like she was *his*. To pretend, even for a few minutes, that she wasn't on the run from a maniac and that she and Logan could actually have something real between them.

"Stormy…" he growled.

"I'm sorry. I just want to be closer."

He made another sexy, guttural sound as he curled his body around hers. One strong thigh slid over hers, and a thick arm circled her chest. His hand cupped her breast as he spooned her. Stella closed her eyes against her mounting desire, acutely aware of his heat, his strength, and his massive erection pressing against her ass. She tried to ignore his hot breath on her neck sending shivers of anticipation through her.

She was not going to get a lick of sleep tonight.

Lick. Hmm.

His hard length felt like a passionate challenge, impossible to resist. She nuzzled against him.

"Stormy." A warning. He tightened his grip and pressed his hips forward.

His conflicting messages made her smile. She trapped her lower lip between her teeth and tried to ward off the urge to tear her panties off and ease down onto him.

Her heart raced.

Sleep. Sleep. Sleep.

His cock twitched against her.

Sleep. Sleep. Sleep.

His lips met the curve of her shoulder, and she felt herself go damp. She tried to convince herself that he was just getting comfortable and his lips had landed there by accident.

He moaned.

Lordy, Lordy.

"I want to make love to you," he whispered.

She forced herself to stay still, because she was worried that if she moved at all, she'd climb on top of him and ride him like a bull. This had to be a test. He was seeing how trustworthy she was. She'd said she wouldn't let him touch her.

"But you said..." Her words drifted into the darkness. She knew what he'd said, and she knew he felt the same bond between them that had started as protector and victim and changed at breakneck speed into so much more.

He shifted her onto her back and gazed into her eyes with so much raw emotion, she lost her ability to speak.

"I don't want to fuck you, Stormy. I want to make love to you. There's a difference. I've never wanted to make love to a woman before. Fuck? Yes. Take? Yes. Make love? Only you, sweetheart. That is, if you want me to." He touched her cheek, and the intimacy of it sparked an immediate and total release of the emotions she'd been trying to deny.

"Yes," she whispered. "Logan..."

"Not a fuck. I don't want to be one in a line of dicks, Stormy. I want you to trust me, to be with me and only me."

"No line...God, Logan. I haven't even been with a guy in months. I've been trying to push away my feelings for you and remain strong, but I can't. They're too much. Too real."

He searched her eyes, and she knew as he slanted his lips over hers and kissed her tenderly that he saw the real her breaking through as strongly as she felt it. Everything about the way he kissed her, the way his hands moved over her, was different. He was caressing instead of groping, as if he were touching her for the first time. He gently removed her shirt, raining kisses down her neck, over her breasts, and then he came up and loved her mouth again. She'd never been touched like this. She felt special, cherished, and it had been so long since she'd *been* herself that she didn't know what to do with the emotions burning inside her.

His hands played gingerly over her ribs as he kissed his way south, lingering around her belly button, placing enticing kisses low on her belly. She wanted him to go lower, wanted to feel his mouth on her, his tongue inside her, but he was moving up her body again, torturing her in the most delicious way. Lapping each taut nipple, heightening her anticipation with every slick of his tongue, every touch of his hands. She felt the facade she'd been hiding behind slipping away. He was breaking through the prickly persona she'd worn like a coat, quieting the fear Kutcher had instilled in her and reawakening deeper emotions she'd long ago buried.

"You're so beautiful, Stormy."

Stormy. Guilt threaded through her. He wasn't Kutcher or someone who was out to hurt her, and she was still treating him like he was. He gripped her hips and kissed the tops of her thighs, looping his finger into her panties and dragging them down, leaving her bare beneath his glorious body. He splayed his hands over her thighs. The heat of his calloused palms seeped into her bones as he brought his mouth to her center. She bucked against his mouth with the first flick of his tongue over her sensitive flesh. He tightened his grip on her legs, tucking them beneath his arms, against his muscular sides, and lifting her hips off the mattress, allowing him better access to drive her out of her freaking mind.

When he sank his fingers deep inside her, her toes curled under.

"Ah, you like that," he said before sinking his teeth into her inner thigh.

She gasped. "Logan…"

"Did I hurt you?"

"God, no. Please, more, Logan. More."

His lips quirked up with a devilish grin. "Don't worry, baby. I'll get you there."

His mouth came down again while his fingers played over the spot that made her blood hotter, heavier, and her breaths shallow. Waves of pleasure rolled down her spine, through her limbs. He teased that spot over and over. She came hard and fast, infused with shocks that radiated through her chest. He lapped and loved her through the very last wave of pleasure. He must have slipped off his briefs, because when he sealed his lips over hers, she felt the wide tip of his arousal pressing against her wet center.

Jesus, everything felt bigger with Logan, better, more real. And if there was one thing Stella wanted, it was *real*. She clutched at his biceps, and her stomach fluttered. She didn't just want real. She wanted *Logan*.

Guilt felt like a wall standing between them.

"Wait, Logan."

LOGAN KNEW HE'D taken a chance by opening himself up to Stormy, but he couldn't resist. Now the fear in her eyes nearly flattened him. Had she not wanted this? Had he scared her off? If this wasn't real, he knew for a fact that he'd *never* know what real felt like.

"Wait." Her voice softened.

Her hands slid down his arms, and he felt hope slipping away. They came to rest on his cheeks. God, he loved her touch.

"Stormy, I'm sorry. I didn't mean to—"

She pressed one finger to his lips. "Shh. You didn't do anything wrong, Logan. You did everything right." She smiled up at him, and he saw her remaining walls come crumbling down. "My name is Stella. Stella Krane."

He let out a breath he hadn't realized had been caught in his throat and dropped his forehead to hers. She trusted him, and in doing so, she righted everything that had felt wrong with his world since his father died.

"Stella. I'm falling hard for you, Stella Krane."

A trickle slipped from the corner of her eye. He kissed the salty tears, then lowered his mouth to hers as their bodies joined together. He buried himself deep, perched above the woman who opened his heart and made him feel again.

Logan had never felt so alive or so vulnerable.

Stella rocked her hips, and he pressed in deeper, keeping her still.

"I just want to feel you wrapped around me for a minute."

"Yes." Her legs circled his waist, locked at the ankles.

He moved slowly at first, eking out every second of loving her he could. Logan reared up, drinking in the flush on her chest, the sheen of sweat on her brow. Her eyes darkened as he thrust in deep. She frantically clutched at the sheets, fighting her release.

"More, Logan. God, give me more."

He gently turned her onto her stomach and lifted her onto her knees, kissing the hollow at the base of her spine, teasing her clit, weighing what she really wanted from him. How far she wanted this to go.

"Take me, Logan. I can't wait any longer."

She pressed her ass back as he entered her wet center. He wanted everything with Stella. He wanted to climb into her skin and experience every emotion she did. He wanted to make her feel things she'd never felt before, but mostly he wanted her to feel safe every second they were together.

He pressed his chest to her back and nibbled the shell of her ear. "I want to touch you, Stella. I want to touch your ass."

"Yes." One long, heated breath.

"You're sure?"

"God, Logan. I want this. I want you."

He kissed his way down her spine, his heart racing with anticipation, full with emotion. He spread her cheeks and teased her hole with his thumb, earning a sweet, sexy moan. She moved in time to each hard thrust as he taunted, but he didn't enter her ass. It was too much to resist. He was afraid she'd change her mind, and there was no going back. He gripped her hips and drove his cock into her center deeper.

"Keep touching me, Logan. I love when you do that."

His slick chest met her back as he reached around to her mouth. She sucked his fingers, nearly making him come. He slid one wet finger into her tightest orifice and felt her sex go impossibly tighter. A heady groan escaped his lungs as he reached around her waist with his other hand to stroke the secret spot he knew she loved. She pressed back, taking his finger in deeper.

"Ohgodohgod. Logan."

She panted, rising up and bringing them as close as two people could get. Her head fell back as the orgasm tore through her, claiming her, pulsating around Logan's hard shaft. He wrapped his arms around her as she seated herself fully on his lap, her inner muscles still claiming them both.

"God, Logan. That was…" She panted. "Amazing."

He gathered her hair over one shoulder and kissed the back

of her neck.

"I want you on top of me so I can watch you come."

He lifted her easily by the waist, lay on his back, then lowered her onto his slick erection.

"Oh, God." She pressed her palms to his chest as she rode him. "You feel so good."

"Good doesn't even come close…"

It took all his focus to keep from coming. She was so beautiful, opening up to him, riding him, becoming one with him. He couldn't wait another second; had to see her come so he could give in to the mounting pressure of his own release. He pulled her down on top of him and kissed her hard.

"Come for me again."

He sucked one breast into his mouth while squeezing her other nipple between his index finger and thumb.

"Ohgodohgodohgod."

He brought his hand between her legs and stroked her the way she loved. She gripped his shoulders and slammed her eyes shut as she spiraled over the edge. He swept her beneath him mid-orgasm and drove into her hard and fast, prolonging her orgasm and taking him right up to the edge. His balls tightened, and his body flashed hot as he ground out her name—*Stella*—and surrendered to his own intense release.

Chapter Ten

STELLA AWOKE TO an empty bed, a full heart, and a head full of worry. Last night she'd felt closer to Logan than she'd ever felt to anyone, but would it be weird with him today? What if he regretted opening up to her?

The bed is empty. Of course he regrets it.

She knew it was too much to hope for, to be normal again. To allow herself to feel something for a man again. Rational thinking went out the door as hatred for Kutcher pushed her insecurities, which had magnified over the last few months, to the surface, convoluting her thoughts. Worry turned to disappointment, which quickly turned to anger.

She threw the blankets off and stomped into the bathroom, where she found fresh towels and all of her personal items unpacked.

Hm.

That was a sweet gesture for a guy who regretted being with her.

She showered and came out of the bathroom wrapped in a plush towel and knelt beside her bags. Logan came into the room and sat on the edge of the bed.

"I already unpacked for you. I hope you don't mind, but I figured it might make you more comfortable." He was shirtless, wearing a pair of faded jeans that rode dangerously low on his hips.

"Oh." She rose, and he reached for her, drawing her down to his lap. "Thank you."

He had an easy smile—definitely not the look of a man who was using her. He looked more relaxed than she'd ever seen him.

"You okay?" He brushed her wet hair from her shoulder.

"Uh-huh." Hope swelled inside her, and when fear tried to quell it, she forced that fear aside. She'd felt enough disappointment in her life. She wanted to enjoy this, to allow herself to feel happy again.

"Embarrassed about last night?"

"No. I'm just really nervous." She might as well get all her fears out in the open; otherwise however long they were together would suck.

"Stella—"

"Wait. You don't have to say it. I know. Last night was a fluke. We got caught up in the heat of the moment. I get it."

"Sweetheart, is that how you feel?" The tone was soft, but she saw the muscles in his jaw jump.

"Is...isn't that what you were going to say?" Why was she speaking so softly?

"No." His baby blues pierced a path straight to her heart. "I don't say things I don't mean. I don't do things I don't want to. If I had wanted to fuck you, I'd have fucked you." He looked away, his eyes filled with confusion. "Maybe I suck at this. I've never felt for anyone what I feel for you, so maybe that felt like fucking to you, but to—"

"No. No, that wasn't...*that* at all." She couldn't even say *fuck* right now. Before meeting Kutcher, she'd hardly ever sworn. She hadn't realized until this very second how much of herself Kutcher had stolen.

"Logan, I feel it, too. But something is happening to me. I don't understand it, and I don't know how to describe it, but..." She pressed her lips together, trying to figure out how to explain what she was feeling. "The person I was before Kutcher isn't the same one I am now, or at least not completely. I know that sounds crazy, but when we were together that first time at my apartment, that was the girl I became with Kutcher."

"I understand." His eyes were filled with compassion, but his jaw was still tight.

"No. I worry you don't, and a guy like you..." She dragged her eyes down his impressive physique, feeling like she'd better memorize it quickly, because like everything else good in her life, it probably wouldn't last long. Some sexy chick who liked to *fuck* could take him away in a hot second.

"A guy like you would get bored with the real me."

He drew his brows together. "Bored? Nothing about you is easy or boring." He kissed her softly. "Stella. I love that you trust me enough to share your real name with me."

"You probably already knew it."

"Yes, but you gave it to me, and that means you trust me. At least a little."

She looked up at the ceiling and groaned. "A lot. That's the problem."

"Stella, just spit it out. What's bothering you?"

"I'm not who you think I am," she said before she could chicken out.

"You're not Stella Krane?"

"No! I'm not a girl who says *fuck me* to a guy. I'm not a girl who blows a guy she just met. I was trying to shed my fear. You know, to *break away*, lose myself in lust. I was trying to erase the past."

"Stella, you can't erase the past. The past happened. Trust me, I've tried to erase the past for years, and no matter what, the goddamn past is still there."

"I know…"

"Do you? Because if you do, then you have to also know that I accept your past. I want to help you move forward from your past. I want to put away the asshole who made your past take over your present." His face tightened. "I want to kill him, but I won't because that wouldn't allow me to be part of your future."

"My…Logan." She could hardly believe the things he was saying, but his voice, the way his eyes filled with sincerity, and her *heart*, were telling her that this was real and that Logan was a good man. An honest man.

She was done being someone she wasn't. She wanted Logan to know the real Stella Krane. The one she was proud of, the one she hoped could still return. The Stella Krane who wanted to bring him home to meet her mother.

"There's more. I want you to know how far I am from being the person I used to be. You know that guy in the bar? The one I know you heard me tell to go home and *fuck* his wife?" She covered her face, her cheeks burning with shame. She hadn't wanted to say the vile word. She felt his arms circle her waist. "I'm not that girl either."

"Okay, so you don't like to talk dirty." He said this like it was no big deal. As if he'd said, *Okay, so you don't like turkey.* "All these emotions are new for *both* of us, and it scares me shitless, too."

"It does?" She couldn't imagine Logan being scared of anything.

"Yes, but I want this."

"But I'm so messed up."

Logan pressed his lips to hers again. "Kutcher's messed up. You're scared. There's a difference. I will never hurt you, Stella, and I'll never let anyone else lay a hand on you ever again."

She'd forgotten what it felt like to be cared about and to let herself hope. His confidence was arresting and reassuring, and it gave her strength.

"So stop worrying. Clean talk, dirty talk, no talk? It's not the words you use that give them meaning, Stella. It's the emotions driving them."

She felt her cheeks flush. "I like talking dirty with you, but I think I like it when it means *more* than…you know."

"Stella Krane, I want *more* with you. I want everything you're willing to give."

Chapter Eleven

LOGAN DROVE HIS father's old pickup truck down the mountain toward Sweetwater with Stella sitting beside him. He didn't drive his father's truck often, but when he did, it made him feel closer to his father. And now he felt closer to his father and Stella, which made Logan feel good. His father would have liked Stella, and he wished he were alive to meet her.

"Do you miss your dad more when you drive his truck?" Stella asked.

"I miss him all the time, but yeah, I do."

She placed her hand on his thigh and leaned her head on his shoulder.

"What's it like, knowing you can't see him again?"

He knew she was asking because of her mom's cancer, but she hadn't shared that information with him yet, and as with her name, he wanted her to trust him enough to share those most private parts of her life with him. He felt his throat thickening as he prepared to tell her the truth.

"I wake up every day and there's this moment when life seems normal. The sun comes up, and I think about work and what I have to do that day. And then my mind always turns to my mom, and when it does, it hits me anew. Dad's gone." He paused to gain control of the tears that threatened to fall.

"I'm sorry. I didn't mean to upset you," Stella said.

"It's fine, darlin'." He kissed the top of her head. "In those first few seconds as I remember, I feel like I'm being sucked under by a big wave. I can't breathe. I'm not sure which way is up, and my world spins around me. And in the next breath, I stuff it away so I can function again." He let out a fast, hard breath. "I was close to my dad. He didn't want me to join the military. He wanted me home. He wanted me safe. But I had something to prove."

She looked up at him with a curious gaze. "And did you? Prove something, I mean."

He shrugged. "I never knew what it was I was proving. I just knew I needed to fight for my country like other people were."

"Then you did what you set out to do."

She said it so simply, and he'd never thought of it as being simple. He'd been trying to figure out exactly *what* he had to prove. He wasn't proving anything at all. He was doing what he thought was right.

They drove down the long two-lane road toward town. It was a sleepy road lined with meadows on each side.

"My worst fear is that my mom will die before I see her again. She has cancer. She was responding well to the treatments when I left, but I..." She turned away, and he knew she was staving off tears.

"You'll see her again, Stella. I promise." He pulled her closer.

"I hope so. She's strong. That's where I get it from. She's determined to beat it, and I hate that I had to leave, but I was worried he would hurt her."

"I know." He was sure her mother did, too. "What about your father?"

She shrugged. "I never knew him. My mom was only nineteen when she had me, and he took off. It's fine, though. I don't feel like I've missed out by not having a father. My mom more than made up for it. We're so close. I just miss her so much."

Wide cobblestone streets and old-fashioned storefronts came into view.

"Logan, is this Sweetwater?"

He was still trying to tamp down his renewed anger toward Kutcher for forcing her out of her life and away from her mother. "Yeah," he managed.

"I love the way these Victorian houses are painted. They're so colorful. It feels very old-fashioned, the way they're mixed in with the old stores." The excitement in her voice surprised Logan, and then he remembered how practiced she was at moving past her pain and sadness.

He turned inward and cold when he tried to do that, but she somehow maintained her warmth and positive outlook.

"You're a remarkable person, Stella." He kissed her again.

"Hardly."

She pointed at a market with a green awning over the entrance. Family owned markets and boutiques took the place of chain grocery and department stores. Unlike in New York City, most of the residents in Sweetwater had grown up here. They gave meaning to the old saying *It takes a village to raise a child* and carried that forward toward the elderly, the ill, the sad, the happy, and everything in between.

"This is beautiful, but I don't understand why I can't stay at the cabin. You said I was safe there."

Stella had acted hot and cold all morning, as if she vacillated over trusting that his feelings were sincere. Logan felt her hesitation with every layer of armor she peeled away, but he wasn't deterred. The article he'd read about Stella and her mother had painted a picture of a loving daughter who took care of her ailing mother, and as Stella softened toward him, it was easy to reassemble the image of who she'd been. Now he needed to make her world safe, so she could go back to being that person again, and be reunited with her mother.

"I'm not comfortable leaving you alone."

"But you said I was safe. How can I be safer here? Out in the open? What if you're wrong and someone tailed us?"

"We weren't tailed. Have a little faith in me. I *am* a PI, you know." He shook his head and smiled. "You'll enjoy it here."

She smiled as Sugar Lake came into view.

"That's Sugar Lake."

"It's pretty." She laced her fingers with his. "Who's the girl you're handing me off to again?"

Logan parked in front of Sweetie Pie Bakery, owned by Willow Dalton, a friend of Logan's. A bright pink awning gave way to two large picture windows. He cut the engine and faced Stella. Her hair tumbled over her shoulders in waves. She wore a loose turquoise tank top, a pair of jeans, and a wary look in her beautiful eyes.

"I'm not *handing you off.* I'm hoping to give you a few hours of remembering what it was like to live without watching your back. You'll like Willow, and you might get to meet her sister, Bridgette. She owns the Secret Garden florist shop next door."

"How do you know them?"

"I met Willow a few years ago, when I found her skinny-dipping on my property."

"Oh." Jealousy filled that word as she tried to take her hand from his.

Logan held on tight. "She's a *friend,* Stella. Willow's great. You'll love her. In fact, she's a lot like you."

The furrow didn't leave her brow as her eyes rolled skeptically over him. "If she's like me, did you hook up with her?"

"You're cute when you're jealous." Logan smiled as she rolled her eyes. "Believe it or not, I don't sleep with every pretty girl I see. I don't know what makes a person attracted to one person instead of another, but I can assure you, she's like the smart-ass sister I never had, and I've never hooked up with her. More important, you'll like her." Logan had met Willow shortly after his father had died, and although she'd been embarrassed about being caught skinny-dipping, and he'd been angry and still reeling from his father's death, they'd had an instant kinship. She'd seen his sadness and his anger, and rather than run, she'd put her clothes back on and taken a walk with Logan, pulling answers from him like a dentist pulls teeth, one painful moment at a time. Willow's friendship had helped him that weekend, and in the years since, her family had become like a second family to him.

Logan came around to Stella's side of the truck and helped her out. "Sweetheart, you wear tension like a second set of clothes, and for good reason, but..." He pulled her into an embrace. Her body remained rigid against him. He crashed his lips over hers, forcing her mouth open with his tongue in a wet, sloppy kiss that made them both laugh.

She laughed as she wiped her mouth. "That was like a bad Jim Carrey movie kiss."

"Made you relax, didn't it? I'll make it up to you later." He took her very relaxed hand, glad she'd laughed the tension away.

"You bet you will," she mumbled.

Bells sounded above them as they walked into the bakery and were assaulted by an aroma of sugary goodness that made Logan's mouth water.

"Oh my God. I think I want to live here and smell this all day long," Stella said quietly.

Willow's blond head popped up from behind one of the glass displays.

"Logan!" She practically scaled the counter to get to him. He shot a look at the arched entranceway that led to Bridgette's flower shop to see if he'd be mauled from both directions, but he didn't see Bridgette. They loved to double-team him and bowl him over.

"Logan! Honey, I've missed you." Willow threw her arms around him and kissed him smack on the lips, then turned a wide smile to Stella and pulled her into an equally enthusiastic hug. Willow was in her midtwenties and was tall and curvy. She had a big personality rivaled only by the size of her heart. "You must be Stella. You're every bit as pretty as Logan said you were."

"Hi." Stella looked at Logan and mouthed, *You told her I was pretty?*

He shrugged, loving the look of appreciation in her eyes.

Willow took a step back and held Stella's hands. "Honey, Logan doesn't ever bring women around, and I mean *ever*. I was worried the guy would end up alone with a house full of porn, if you know what I mean."

"Hey," Logan protested halfheartedly.

"Not that he doesn't have every girl in this town after him." Willow tossed her thick braid over her shoulder and crossed her arms. "So, I hear Logan has to go do guy things, and you get to spend the day with me. I can't wait to get to know you."

"Thanks, Willow," Logan said.

"Yes, thank you. I won't be any trouble. I could have stayed at his cabin—"

"Nonsense." Willow swatted the air. "First of all, why would you stay in that cabin all by yourself when you could be here with me?" She leaned in close and whispered, "I'm fun, trust me. Did he tell you how we met?"

"Hey, Willow. Don't take her skinny-dipping."

Stella turned mischievous eyes in his direction. God, he loved seeing that spark in her eyes.

"Jealous? Maybe we'll skinny-dip in Sugar Lake." Stella arched a brow.

Logan scrubbed his hand down his face. "What have I done?"

Willow put a muffin in a bag and handed it to Logan. "Go on. Go do your boy things. We'll be fine." She shooed him toward the door.

He reached for Stella and lowered his voice. "You okay? You have the phone I gave you?"

"Actually, I'm fine now. And I have the phone." She hugged him and whispered, "Thank you."

He couldn't resist giving her a soft kiss.

"Oh my goodness. Get out of here before you have her all googly-eyed. I'm gonna get to know this chickadee and make sure you're not too bad of an influence on her. Go." Willow shooed him out again.

BY MIDDAY STELLA felt more comfortable than she had since she left Mystic. Willow was easy to talk to, a good listener, and warm and wonderful with each and every customer that came into the bakery. Each customer had a story to share—news of a pending birth, an upcoming event for a church group, a cousin who had hit hard times. There were too many to keep track of, and Willow listened intently, offered advice, and doled out hugs and well-wishes to nearly everyone. It was easy to see how she and Logan would get along. Two people for whom helping others was stamped in their DNA.

They were baking cookies, something Stella hadn't done in years. It made her long for her mother even more than usual.

"So, how did you end up with Logan? All he told me was that he was trying to track down a bad guy. I swear he's like a modern-day Superman." Willow took a batch of cookies from the oven and slid another tray in.

She felt like she could open up to Willow, and more important, she wanted to. She already felt like a friend, and Stella didn't have many friends these days.

"This is going to sound like I'm a weak, pathetic girl, but really, I'm not." Stella didn't want anyone's pity, and even though she sensed that Willow wouldn't pity her, she still felt the need to clarify.

"Honey, we're all weak girls. You know that saying 'A real woman can do things herself'? Well, I buy into the next part, too. 'But a real man won't let her.' Heck, if I had a man like Logan, I'd get in trouble on purpose just to let him save me."

Stella felt her jaw drop open.

Willow finished rolling out the dough before lifting her eyes to Stella. "Oh God." She wiped her hands on her apron. "I'm not interested in Logan. I didn't mean—"

"No, it's not that." Stella sank into a chair. "I just realized as I was listening to you that I don't even know *how* to act normal anymore. I haven't had a girlfriend to talk to in months, and I don't know how to react to things. Because of my life, I feel like I have to be this tough, bitchy, hard woman. I mean, I do have to or my wacko ex-boyfriend might find me and kill me. *Literally*. But when I hear you talk, I want to be *that* girl again. I want to talk about how fun it would be to be with Logan and how freaking hot he is, and I want so badly for my biggest worry to be if Logan will be late for a date." She felt tears stinging her eyes as Willow crouched beside her.

Stella realized she'd completely spilled her guts without even thinking about it. She was relieved to see empathy in Willow's eyes instead of pity, and she was powerless to stop the truth from coming out. "I don't even know how to classify what we are together. He's rescuing me." As the words left her lips, they felt wrong. But she was afraid to believe in what she felt and what he said he felt. In two more days Kutcher would be out, and God only knew how long it would be before he found her. She couldn't even bear the thought.

"First off, Logan will not let any psycho ex near you, and, honey, this is not how Logan rescues." Willow wrapped her arms around Stella, and Stella couldn't hold back the flood of tears that had been welling inside her for months. "Honey, I've known him for a few years. I've never seen Logan with a woman he cares about, because there haven't been any. He keeps a professional distance from his clients, and he definitely *doesn't* bring them here to Sweetwater."

Willow lightly touched Stella's shoulder. "This is Logan's second hometown. He treasures this place as much as we do. There's only one reason Logan would bring you here. He's not rescuing you, honey. He's falling for you."

Chapter Twelve

BETWEEN THE INFORMATION Logan had been able to gather through his sources yesterday and the calls he made on the way to Connecticut after dropping Stella off with Willow, he knew exactly where to find Bob Kanets. Kanets had spent more time in jail than out in his thirty-eight years. There were smart criminals, the ones who knew how to beat the system, how to cover their asses and let someone else take the fall when the police were hot on their trail. Then there were guys like Kanets. Guys who hung out in back alleys, dealt drugs in broad daylight, and fought like dogs when they were caught, which only drove the nail further into their coffins. He'd gotten out of prison eight weeks ago and had gone right back to the path that had led him there in the first place—drug dealing on the outskirts of Mystic.

Logan sat in the rental car he'd secured when he'd arrived in Mystic, across the street from the abandoned warehouse where Kanets was known for dealing. The place looked like every seedy drug drop depicted in low-budget movies. It was an abandoned redbrick school building with half the windows boarded up, the other half broken out, leaving gaping black holes like missing teeth in an ancient mouth. Ivy snaked across the left side of the building, climbing over and into the holes. Two banged-up air-conditioning units hung from windows on the top floor, sagging and brown with age. Concrete steps led to entrances on opposite ends of the front of the building. From his vantage point, Logan saw a few feet into each entrance. The white interior walls were streaked with filth and colorful graffiti. Half of the steps to the right were buried beneath overgrown weeds. The entrance on the left was free of vegetation but littered with broken glass and cans. He'd already checked out the back of the building, where there was one entrance covered with spiderwebs from the railings to the wall. There was thick dirt, free of footprints, covering the steps. No one had frequented that entrance, at least not anytime recently. He'd been casing the building for an hour and a half. He'd seen two guys go in, and only one had come out. Logan was biding his time.

He checked his phone and assumed no texts from Stella was a good sign. He knew she was in good hands with Willow. Willow and her family had embraced Logan as if he were family, and he knew she'd do the same with Stella.

Stella. She'd appeared in his life out of nowhere and had slithered under his skin without even trying. Fate must have been on his side when he completed his assignment in Memphis early. If he hadn't been in town, God only knew what would have happened to Stella that night at the bar. His skin crawled just thinking about the possibilities.

His phone flashed with a call from an unknown number, but he let it go to voicemail. He needed to remain focused on getting things under control for Stella. He called Marco and confirmed that Winters was still behaving. As he ended the call, the lanky guy with waist-length hair he'd seen enter the building earlier came out. The guy shoved his hands in his pockets and lumbered down the road with his eyes trained on the ground.

Logan checked his gun and slid it into the shoulder holster

beneath the flannel shirt he wore open over a wrinkled T-shirt. He'd changed into his scumbag clothes so as not to stand out. He buried his fingers in his hair and scrubbed. Between his unshaven cheeks, mussed hair, wrinkled clothes, and torn and dirty sneakers, he should fit right in with Kanets's usual prospects. He stepped from the rental car, head bowed, eyes darting, and ducked around the side of the building, which looked as sordid as the front, then entered the building as silently as the wind, heading up the stairs toward the second floor, where he'd seen Kanets earlier through one of the missing windows.

He stole a glance into the room before tucking himself against the wall in the hallway. In two seconds flat he'd taken in Kanets's stringy blond hair, his rail-thin, rounded shoulders, and his lanky body as he paced by the missing window with a pistol in the back of his pants. The room was empty save for a dented metal desk pushed against one wall. It was hardly a gamble that Kanets had drugs on him. Possession of drugs and a weapon while on parole would mean an easy five years minimum.

Logan had made his mark.

He shoved his hands in his pockets, bowed his head, and staggered into the room. Kanets spun around.

"You Kanets?" Logan spoke in a bored drawl.

"Who wants to know?" Kanets's eyes jumped around the room as Logan casually closed the distance between them, shrugging.

"Kutcher sent me." Logan kept his head bent, which went against everything he'd ever been taught, but he knew how to play this scared rat.

"Cool. Can't wait until he's out to take care of his own shit.

Whatchu need?"

"Just some blast, man. Kutcher said you got it." *Blast* was the street term for injectable cocaine powder, which was Kanets's bread and butter.

Kanets lifted his chin toward the desk. "In the drawer."

Logan eyed Kanets's pockets, noting the telltale bulge. He was reasonably sure he had drugs on him, which would make this much easier than trying to nail him with drugs in the room. *Idiot.* Logan walked toward the desk, and as if on cue, Kanets stepped in closer. Logan waited for Kanets to step behind him. In the next second Logan had Kanets's right arm wrenched behind his back, Kanets's face pressed to the top of the metal desk.

"You can thank Kutcher," Logan growled between clenched teeth as he took Kanets's pistol and tucked it into the back of his own pants.

"What the fuck?" Kanets spat.

Logan let him rattle on. He was just dumb enough to hang himself.

"Motherfucker. What's he think? I'm cheatin' him? The asshole."

"He is an asshole." Logan almost felt sorry for Kanets. He was such a dumbass.

"Motherfuckin' right, he's an asshole. I'm not cheatin' him. Take the drugs, man. Take the cash. It's in my pocket. Take it all. I don't give a fuck."

"If I wanted the drugs, you'd be dead and I'd be gone."

"What?" Kanets's voice cracked. "No, no, no. Motherfuck." His body began to shake. "No, man. Don't kill me. I'll get him the cash. Every fucking cent."

Bingo.

"Only a fool would try to scam Kutcher." Logan pressed the muzzle of his gun harder against Kanets's head. Kanets bucked, trying to break free of Logan's vise grip. *Keep trying, prick. You're going nowhere fast.*

"Hey, man. Wait. Wait, man. I got…gotta…idea."

I bet you do.

"I'll give you his money. Yeah, yeah. That's it. The drugs, too. Then you can take off and sell it. It's gotta be more than he's paying you to off me."

"Shut the fuck up. I'm a private investigator. I'm not with Kutcher. I'm nailing him."

"Fuck, man."

"Shut up." This was too easy. He was putty in Logan's hands. "Here's what's gonna happen. I'm going to take you down to the station, and you're going to tell *those* motherfuckers everything you know about Kutcher. The dealing he's doing from the pen, who his customers are, the whole load of shit." After the police had given up looking for his father's killer, Logan had lost a lot of respect for the men in blue, but there was about an ounce left. Enough to know how to play the fucking game when he was in their presence. Beyond that, Logan did things his own way.

"Got it?" Logan twisted his arm to send his message home.

"I'm not going back to jail. No fucking way. You can kill me."

"That's a shame. I kinda liked this T-shirt. Guess I can wash the blood out." He let out a bored breath, and Kanets flailed harder.

"Wait!"

Logan crushed Kanets's face into the desk again. "You fucking ready to play, or you wanna die? My trigger finger is mighty itchy. I'll get you a fucking plea bargain for ratting out Kutcher, but if you fuck up…" Logan leaned down and spoke in a threateningly low tone. "I'll take great pleasure in killing you."

"Fine. Fine. I'll fucking do it."

"Louder. You'll do what?" Logan demanded.

"I'll fucking snitch, man. I'll tell them everything."

"Good boy, because possession of drugs and a firearm while on parole is some nasty shit. And this…" He tapped Kanets's head with his gun. "This is the only alternative you've got."

Chapter Thirteen

STELLA BOXED A dozen muffins for a customer and rang up her purchase. After she'd bared her soul to Willow, which she'd followed with a brief wallow in embarrassment, Stella had been forced to find her footing again. Willow hadn't allowed her to wallow for more than a few minutes. She had set her hands on her ample hips, leveled a determined stare at Stella, and said, *Honey, you've got a wicked hot man out there fighting for your life, a funny chick standing right here, ready to have some fun, and you want to waste your energy on being embarrassed? You go right ahead, but I'm going to eat a cupcake.* She proceeded to take the biggest bite Stella had ever seen of a white cupcake with pink frosting. After finishing that one, Willow had licked each finger and grabbed another.

"You'd better get yours fast. Otherwise they'll all be gone. Trust me, this girl knows how to eat." Willow ate half of the second cupcake in one bite and then flashed a toothy smile.

That was several hours ago, and since then Stella had been having so much fun helping customers and baking that she'd almost forgotten about Kutcher. *Almost.* The problem was she definitely hadn't forgotten about Logan, and every time her mind drifted to him, she remembered where he was. And then she'd feel a little queasy, until the bakery got busy again and sidetracked her thoughts.

After Stella rang up the muffins, she went to help a young couple who was waiting, but Willow came out of the kitchen, patted her shoulder as she whizzed by, and beat her to it. Now, with a moment to think, Stella's mind turned back to Logan. He hadn't told her what he was going to do. *Important PI stuff* could mean anything. She envisioned him with all sorts of expensive equipment, scoping out…What? Kutcher was in jail, due to get out in two days. Her stomach sank again. She had no idea what Logan was doing, but she'd seen him carry two duffel bags to the truck when they were getting ready to leave. She hoped that whatever it was, he was safe.

A tall blond woman with wild curls flew through the doors, sending the bells above the doors into a frenzy. She wore a billowy long skirt and a fitted top that made her appear younger than her wise eyes conveyed.

"Wow! What a glorious day!" The woman set a box on the counter with a loud *thump* and pushed her springy curls from her face. She narrowed her eyes at Stella, shifted a curious gaze to Willow, then back to Stella.

"That's Stella, Mom," Willow said from where she was bent over behind the counter, plucking cookies from the display and boxing them for the couple.

Mom?

Willow's mother's eyes widened, and a warm smile appeared.

"Oh, honey." She motioned for Stella to come around the counter. "Come over here. Let me see you." Willow obviously came by her high energy naturally.

Stella stepped nervously around the counter. She had a feeling she was in for scrutiny and wasn't sure she was up for it, even with all the fun she'd had with Willow.

"Hi, Mrs. Dalton. I'm…" She hesitated out of habit, and realized Willow already knew her real name and she'd already revealed it to her mother. Logan must really trust them to have shared her true identity. She wasn't sure why that hadn't clicked earlier. Probably because Willow had instantly made her feel comfortable.

"Stella Krane. It's nice to meet you."

Willow's mom waved a dismissive hand. "*Pfft.* Call me Roxie, honey. The only one allowed to call me Mrs. Dalton is…Well, I can't think of a darn soul around here." She tugged Stella into a hug, crushing her so hard against her chest that she could barely breathe.

"So you're Logan's girl. Nice man, that Logan Wild." She took Stella's hand and led her to one of the tables by the window.

Stella stole a glance at Willow, ringing up the couple's purchase. Willow shrugged and smiled, as if this was how life was around here. Stella shifted uncomfortably in her seat. *Logan's girl?* What had he told them?

Roxie leaned across the table and took Stella's hands in her own. "Oh, sugar. What is that trouble I see brewing in your eyes?"

Am I that transparent?

Roxie patted Stella's hand. The couple left the bakery, making the bells sound again. Stella looked at the door, over at Willow, anywhere except into the eyes of the warm, friendly mind reader sitting across from her.

"Don't tell me, sugar. Just know that whatever it is, if you need to talk, Willow and I are here. Any friend of Logan's is a friend of ours."

Willow stood beside the table holding the box her mother

had set on the counter. "Mom, I have enough soap. I'll share it with Bridge."

Roxie released Stella's hands and rose to her feet. "Nonsense. You can never have enough soap."

Willow rolled her eyes. "My mom makes her own soap and other incredibly delicious-smelling lotions and fragrances."

"Did I see Mom's car?" Another tall blonde, with a little boy perched on her hip, came through the archway that led from the flower shop. Stella quickly realized it was Bridgette, Willow's older sister. Willow had raved about Bridgette and her three-year-old son, Louie. The only similarities between the sisters were their friendly smiles and their green eyes. Bridgette's shoulder-length hair was wavy and thick with multiple shades of blond and brown, while Willow's was as blond as blond could be, and her braid hung almost to her waist.

"There's my little pumpkin." Roxie reached for Louie.

"Grandma Roxie!" He wrapped his lithe arms around her neck and hugged her with all his might. Roxie glanced over her shoulder at Stella. "Nice to meet you, Stell. I'm going to take my boy into the flower shop and see what he's been up to in there."

Stella felt a pang in her heart at the scene unfolding before her. She longed to see her mother, to know how she was feeling and to feel her arms around her.

No sense pining over something I might never be able to do again.

As she'd done so many times before, she tucked thoughts of her mother away and focused on Willow and her family. Bridgette was less animated and much leaner than curvy Willow, though they were both equally beautiful.

Bridgette reached into the box, and Willow turned the box

away from her with a mischievous smile.

"Willow!" Bridgette smiled at Stella and rolled her eyes, like this was a familiar battle. "Hi. I'm Bridgette, and that little monkey was my son, Louie."

Stella returned the smile. "Hi, I'm Stella. A friend of Logan's."

Bridgette and Willow exchanged a glance that told of sisterly secrets. Stella felt a pang of longing again. She was envious of the energy between the two girls, and it made her long for friendships again. She'd become an expert at ignoring her loneliness, but being here with Willow today brought it all to the forefront.

Bridgette set an assessing gaze on her.

"What?" Stella asked with a hint of confusion.

"Logan doesn't bring *friends* here," Bridgette said. "We've met one of his hot brothers, but otherwise, he comes alone."

"She's his girlfriend," Willow said with an air of confidence. When Stella opened her mouth to respond, Willow handed the box of soap to Bridgette and held a palm up to Stella. "Don't even try to deny it."

"I'm not getting in the middle of this, but you could do a lot worse than Logan. He's the nicest guy around, and easy on the eyes, too." Bridgette glanced in the box. "Take what you want and I'll put the rest in the pantry so we can share them, Will."

Willow plucked a few bars of soap from the box. The door opened behind them, and they all turned. Logan's eyes zeroed in on Stella. Her pulse quickened as he placed his hand on her hip, and pressed his lips to hers. She stole a glance at Willow and Bridgette, and they were both smiling.

They looked at each other and said in unison, "Definitely

his girlfriend."

Stella felt her cheeks heat up and caught Logan's confident—*proud?*—gaze. The idea that he would be proud to be with her made her stomach do that flippy thing again.

"Was there a bet placed, and if so, who lost?" Logan's lips quirked up in a devilish grin.

"She lost." Bridgette nodded to Stella before hugging Logan. "Good to see you."

Louie came barreling into the bakery with Roxie on his heels. "Logan!" The little bundle of energy flung himself into Logan's arms.

"Hey, buddy. How's it going?" Everything about Logan softened as his arms circled the boy in a protective and loving embrace.

"Did you bring me anything?" Louie asked.

Bridgette touched her son's back. "Louie, that's not nice."

"But he always brings me things," Louie said as he touched Logan's cheek with his pudgy little hand. "Don't ya?"

Logan shifted his eyes to Bridgette, silently waiting for approval, and that thoughtful motion made Stella's heart open to him even more. He was so different from the man she'd thought he was when she'd first seen him, and it made her realize how similar they were. Both appearing to be something they weren't. As she watched Logan give Louie a pack of baseball cards he'd had hidden in his pocket and then crouch beside the boy as he opened them, Stella wanted to know everything about Logan. How was he so fearless when he obviously had an equally strong nurturing, loving side? Why was their connection so powerful? And what had he done today that made him look so relaxed?

"Come on, buddy. We have to get back to the flower shop,"

Bridgette said as she took Louie's hand. They said goodbye to Stella and Logan and disappeared the way they'd come.

Logan placed a hand on Stella's lower back as if it were the most natural thing in the world. She moved closer, beginning to believe it was. Logan smiled as he slid his hand around her waist to tighten his hold.

"Thank you for letting Stella spend the day here," Logan said to Willow.

"We had fun, didn't we, Stella?"

Stella nodded, trying to ignore the quick and disturbing thoughts that were rushing into her mind. There were fewer than forty-eight hours until Kutcher was released. She'd been able to escape it today amid the busyness of the bakery, but now there was no forcing reality away. She wanted to pretend, just for a while longer, that everything was okay. That she was a normal girl who lived a normal life like she'd done today. She wanted just a few more hours in this friendly town before she slipped into her coat of fear again.

LOGAN SAT ACROSS from Stella in a cozy restaurant at the edge of town, trying to read the conflicting emotions washing over her face. She hadn't eaten much of her dinner and was pushing vegetables across her plate with her fork.

"So, do you really think this guy Kanets will rat out Kutcher? I still don't understand how it can help. Kutcher's getting out of jail, remember?"

Logan reached across the table for her hand, then thought better of it and came around the booth to join her on the bench seat. He draped an arm over her shoulder and pulled her in close, needing to ease her worry but knowing he couldn't guarantee a damn thing.

"I've taken every measure to make him talk, and if he doesn't talk, then he'll go to jail for an even longer time for possession of drugs and firearms while on parole."

"If he's going to jail anyway, why would he rat Kutcher out?" Stella trapped her lower lip between her teeth.

"Because he'll go for many more years without a plea bargain. A day in jail is like a month in the free world. Have faith in me, Stella." Logan cupped her cheek and rubbed his thumb over her lower lip. She followed it with her tongue.

He nuzzled against her cheek. "I missed you so much today. If you keep looking sexy and cute, I'm going to have to kiss you, and I may not stop with one kiss."

"I missed you, too, and I hate when you stop with just one kiss."

Their lips met in an urgent, demanding kiss. He slid his hand up her thigh beneath the cover of the table and swallowed the sweet moan that escaped her lungs. She grabbed his wrist and moved his hand higher. Heat permeated the rough denim. He buried his other hand in her hair and brought his mouth to her ear.

"I want to be inside you." His tongue followed the shell of her ear, and he sucked her sensitive lobe into his mouth. He'd thought about her all day, and the prolonged anticipation was unbearable. He wanted her in his arms, naked beneath him.

Logan stole a quick look toward the front of the almost empty restaurant. He took her in another ravishing kiss and couldn't wait a second longer. He slid from the booth and pulled her up to her feet, dragging her into the narrow hallway in the back of the restaurant that led to the restrooms and trapped her against the wall. Their mouths met in another punishing kiss. His cock throbbed as she arched into him and guided his hand between her legs again.

"Jesus, Stella. You want this," he growled. A thread of guilt snaked into his body, and he pulled back. She was breathing hard; one hand clutched his ass, the other, his chest. He wasn't going to be one of those guys who made her feel cheap or used, and he wasn't going to force himself on her.

"Baby, tell me what you want. Want to go back to the cabin? Want me to back off? What do you want, darlin'?" He drew back a few inches, and she pulled him in closer.

"Bathroom." She felt for the door with her hand, then dragged *him* by his shirt into the men's room.

Logan locked the door and backed her up against the wall.

"You're sure?" he asked against her lips.

"Shut up and kiss me."

Their mouths crashed together again. She fumbled with his jeans as he tore hers open and thrust his hand beneath her panties. She took his throbbing erection in her hand as he dipped his fingers between her legs.

"Oh, *fuck*, darlin'. You're so damn wet."

He thrust his tongue in her mouth as he drove his fingers into her velvety heat, and she worked him with her hand. He used his thumb to get her to the edge, wanting to make her come before he was inside her. Within seconds her head dropped back and her eyes closed. He captured her cries of pleasure in his mouth.

"That's my girl."

He tugged her jeans down and lifted her easily into his arms and lowered her onto his throbbing cock.

"Christ, you feel good."

"Logan." His name came out as a plea.

"Hold on to my shoulders."

She did, and he drove in hard, one powerful thrust after another, as she dug her nails into him.

"Harder, Logan. Fuck me harder."

"Oh, darlin'."

He lifted her off his aching shaft and turned her to face the sink, nudging her legs out wider. The shapely beauty of her creamy ass nearly took him over the edge. He dropped to his knees, had to taste her sweet honey before he entered her again. He spread her cheeks with his hands and thrust his tongue into her slick folds.

"Oh God. Logan."

He licked her swollen sex until her breathing quickened and he could tell she was on the verge of release. In one swift move, he rose to his full height and drove his hard cock into her. Holding her shoulders for balance, he pumped and ground, taking her roughly, unable to hold back another second. They both wanted it. Hell, they both needed it. She was every bit as dirty as he was, only her naughtiness was cocooned in love, and he'd make damn sure that he loved the hell out of her—forever if she'd let him.

"Logan," she cried out, clawing at the countertop.

He thrust as her inner muscles contracted. Heat gathered low in his gut, mounting, thickening, taunting. Another deep thrust pulled him under, and he grunted through his own intense release.

When the last shudder of pleasure rippled through him, he gathered her in his arms and held her close. She gazed into his eyes with the look of trust he'd seen late last night and again this morning. Every time their eyes connected, his heart turned over in his chest. Logan knew this was real. As real as anything he'd ever known. As real as taking down the enemy on his SEAL missions. As real as killing his father's murderer. Adrenaline coursed through him, as it had during all those other times, along with something deeper, something that filled the holes those other things had left behind. Overtaking the shadows of his past and giving him hope for the future.

He helped Stella with her jeans, then righted his own, before pressing a long kiss to her forehead and taking her beautiful face in his hands. Logan was done struggling to keep his feelings in check. He couldn't resist—didn't want to deny—telling her how he felt.

"I love you, Stella. And no matter what the cost, I'll keep you safe."

She closed her eyes for a beat, and the air between them shifted, grew colder. Her jaw tightened. Her grip on his arm eased, and she looked away.

"Don't love me, Logan. I can't stand to lose you, too."

"Stell—"

She was out the door before he could say another word.

Chapter Fourteen

THEY DROVE BACK to the cabin in silence. Stella was lost in a private, torturous battle. She thought she could allow herself to love Logan. She felt everything he felt. When he was making love to her, claiming her with all his might and passion, she wanted to tell him she loved him, too. There was no denying their powerful connection. But she couldn't deny that tomorrow would leave her only twenty-four hours before Kutcher was out of jail again, and she refused to let Logan love her when she might not be around to love.

She felt Logan's eyes on her as she stared out the window into the darkness. She couldn't muster the courage to look at him. He read her better than anyone had ever read her in her life. He knew when she needed to be held, when to let her cry, when to love her hard. She knew he loved her because she felt it in every touch, every kiss, saw it in every look. With Logan she could be herself without any masks or costumes, without any false bravado. With Logan she felt whole, but that wasn't fair to him.

When he parked at the cabin, she rushed out her door so he couldn't open it for her. She knew she'd have to look into his eyes, and she couldn't bear to see the sadness that had gathered there when he'd climbed into the truck at the restaurant. If she did, she'd fall into their love and forget who she was again, and that was too dangerous. Not the person she used to be, the one Logan was quickly unveiling, but the person she'd been for the past few months. The ruined girl. Kutcher's prey.

He didn't reach for her as he strode up the steps. The rounding of his shoulders told of his sorrow. How did she have the power to crush such a strong man? More importantly, how would she survive another day when her own heart was shattering inside her chest? Maybe she'd get lucky and die of a broken heart. That was preferable to dying at the hands of Kutcher.

Logan tossed his keys on the counter and sank into a chair without turning on the lights.

Good.

Darkness was a mask.

She needed a full-on costume to get through tonight.

He ran both hands through his hair and tipped his head back with a sigh.

Stella didn't know what to do, where to sit, where to stand. Her legs felt like lead, and she felt broken.

"I know I'm not being fair to you." She hadn't planned the words, but they came as if she had, with an air of truth. When Logan didn't open his eyes or look in her direction, she continued. "You've turned your life inside out for me, Logan, and you've been so good to me." *Too good to me.*

He crossed his arms, knees spread wide, and dropped his chin to his chest, setting a piercing stare on the coffee table.

She wanted him to turn those eyes on her. How could she miss what wasn't hers? She was the one pushing him away, and she wanted desperately to see him smile again, to see the fire in his eyes that had been there for the past two days.

Instead, she was answered with silence and a clenched jaw.

She swallowed the urge to hide beneath the blankets in the other bedroom and hunker down for a long, cold winter like a bear in the woods.

"I dropped my guard, Logan." Her voice sounded fragile. An hour ago it would have drawn him to his feet and he'd have taken her in his arms and told her that everything would be okay. But he'd bared his soul and she'd turned her back on him. The realization made her weak. She sank onto the couch on the opposite side of the room.

"I allowed myself to get too close to you, but that isn't fair, and I'm sorry. You don't deserve that." Stella fought the urge to push aside what could happen and apologize to Logan. To give herself up to him completely. To lie beneath him and let him love her heart back into one piece. To curl up in his arms, borrow his strength, believe his words, and allow herself to be loved the way she used to hope to be loved—the way she'd allowed herself to dream about being loved by Logan. The picket-fence type of love.

"What was that in the restaurant, Stella? Were you just fucking another guy? Because you told me that wasn't who you were." His voice was dead calm, but his words cut like a knife.

"No. I swear, Logan. I felt everything you felt."

Logan fell into silence again, his jaw working over her words.

"Don't you see? I let myself pretend. I got carried away with my feelings for you and the safety I've been feeling, and I let myself hope. Hope is a dangerous thing. I allowed myself to forget who I was, what my life was really like. There were times today when I felt normal."

She scoffed at her stupidity. "*Normal.* Like I could live in that friendly little town and not fear for my life. Like I could be friends with people like Willow and Bridgette and maybe one day have a family of my own."

She pressed her fist to the pain in her chest, which was burning hotter with every admission.

"I can't do those things, Logan. Kutcher will get out of jail and he'll track me down. And this time he'll probably kill me." Trembling began in her limbs. She choked on her admission. "He…He stabbed me, Logan. Twice. He's not going to quit. He's going to hunt me down until I'm out of his way, and you of all people don't deserve to live like this. You're a good, honest, kind, loving man. You deserve a woman whose life isn't fucked up beyond repair. A woman who knows that in two days she'll still be alive and able to live a normal life."

He rose to his feet. When he tilted his chin in her direction, his features turned to stone. "You don't need to have *hope*, Stella. Hope's for people who can't do a damn thing to make their life better. All you need is to have faith in me." He took a step toward his bedroom, then stopped and spoke with his back to her.

"I'm having dinner with my family tomorrow night. You're coming with me. It's not a request or an option. It's what you're doing so I can keep you safe. You don't have to let me love you. You don't even have to like me. But I'm seeing this through. I'm keeping you safe. Once we know Kutcher's remaining behind bars, you'll get your life back. Whatever life you choose."

He disappeared into his bedroom. Dinner with his family? He was having dinner with his family and she was supposed to go with him? What about Kutcher? What if Kanets didn't talk? What if Kutcher hired someone to hurt her instead of doing it himself? No, she couldn't even let herself think about that now.

It was one thing to facilitate drug sales while he was in jail, but another to hire someone to kill her.

She really was losing her mind.

And now she'd lost Logan, too.

Chapter Fifteen

I SHOULDN'T HAVE touched her.

I shouldn't have made love to her in the bathroom.

Logan had berated himself all night after checking in with Marco and the guys down at the police station and learning that Kanets had caved. That's what Logan had counted on. Now it was up to the system to do the right thing, keep Kutcher behind bars while they investigate and eventually find him guilty and extend his sentence. As much as Logan wanted to blow through the doors of the station and demand that they finish what he started, he knew better. It was time to wait it out and keep Stella safe. They had to be in the city tonight for dinner with his family, but he didn't want Stella there any longer than necessary. He debated skipping dinner, but after his father died, he'd promised himself he'd never blow off a night with his mother for anything. Logan always kept his promises.

After a shitty night, he and Stella had managed to be cordial this morning, navigating the tension that stilted their small talk over breakfast. He loved her so damn much he ached all over. Being in the same room with her was torture. She looked as distraught as he felt, and he'd had to escape to the porch just to have enough oxygen to breathe. He returned phone calls to distract himself from the trouble between them, and he went over his notes on Kutcher again to make sure he hadn't missed anything. Logan never missed things.

But now, hours later, after piddling around in the yard to kill time and chopping more wood than he could ever need, he missed the hell out of Stella. He missed her laugh, the sound of her voice, the feel of her fingers in his.

Shadows crept over his back as the afternoon sun dipped below the tree line. Logan brought the ax down hard, splitting the slab of wood right down the center with a loud *crack*. His body glistened with the effort. He set up another log and stood back, planting his legs into the earth and swinging the ax for the hundredth time that afternoon. It had yet to touch the frustration coiled in every one of his muscles.

He glanced at the cabin and considered apologizing to Stella for taking things too far last night in the restaurant, but hadn't he given her a chance to back out? He hadn't been too full of lust to forget that, but he had obviously been too full of love to misconstrue what last night meant to her, despite what she'd claimed. He'd been making love; she'd been fucking.

He swung the ax again, and the sound of splitting wood echoed in the forest, mirroring the shattering of his heart. He didn't believe she'd been just fucking. She'd said she felt everything he'd felt, and he wanted to believe that. But why would she tear them apart? Why was she trying to protect him? He didn't need protecting. He needed her.

He wiped his sweaty hands on his fatigues and set his boots solidly on the ground again, unable to shake the feeling that none of this shit felt right. It hadn't felt like she was just fucking him last night, no matter what words they'd used, where, or how they'd come together. He wasn't so messed up that he could have misread her, was he?

He split another log, then rested the ax on his shoulder and wiped his brow with his forearm. None of it mattered. Not why she didn't love him or why he loved her. All that mattered was keeping her safe. It had to be a mission now, nothing more. And it probably should have been one all along.

He'd fucked up. That was the bottom line. He knew better than to get involved with someone he was protecting, and before Stella he'd been damn good at staying on the right side of that line.

His phone rang. He pulled it out of his pocket and smiled at his brother's name on the screen. He needed the distraction.

"Hey, Coop. How's it going?"

"Just wrapped a photo session with none other than Siena Remington—you know that hotter-than-fuck model?" Logan's brothers Jackson and Cooper ran one of the most prestigious photography businesses around. They were always shooting famous models and actors.

"The Captain Morgan girl?"

"Yeah, she's the one. Came with her firefighter fiancé. He was cool, though. I actually pulled him into the shoot. It was hot."

"Cool. You going to Mom's for dinner?"

"'Course. That's why I'm calling. Can you cover cooking tonight? I can't get over there early enough."

"Sure. I'm at my cabin, but I'll be there."

Stella came out the front door wearing a pair of jeans and a tight tank top. Their eyes caught—and held—blazing a familiar path between them. Logan didn't drop his gaze. The longer they remained connected, the harder it was to break away—and the deeper her denial cut.

He tore his eyes away, mumbling a curse.

"Did you just curse at me?" Cooper asked.

"No. Just nicked my finger. I'll be there."

"Cool. Thanks, man," Cooper said. "I owe you one."

Logan shoved his phone in his pocket and paced, willing himself not to look at Stella. No wonder he'd kept his heart on ice for so long. This sucked.

He heard the sound of dry leaves crackling beneath her feet but didn't turn to greet her. He wasn't going to make the same mistake twice. The ball was in her court, and it was going to stay there until she made up her mind whether she wanted him or not. He couldn't play the half-in, half-out game any longer. Logan wanted a committed relationship or nothing.

"I want to have faith in you, but I'm so scared." Her voice slid over his skin and melted the ice he needed around his heart in order to remain detached. She placed a delicate hand on his arm and walked in front of him, looking up through impossibly long lashes. Her eyes were red-rimmed. She'd been crying.

His heart broke a little more.

"Wanting is a start." He was putty in her hands. He wanted to be hers.

"I'm sorry. It's not easy for me. Yesterday…when we—"

"I shouldn't have touched you like that. I made you feel dirty and cheap, and it was a prick move. I was satisfying my own greediness for you. I just…" He ran a hand through his hair to try to figure out why she had the power to melt his soul to liquid. "I'm sorry."

"You gave me a choice, Logan." Her tone was cold and exact.

"And you chose to *fuck* me. I get it, Stella." He swung the ax blade into the tree trunk he was using as a mount and headed for the cabin.

"Yes, Logan," she called after him. "I *chose* to fuck you."

Her words shouldn't sting. He was a man, a soldier. He shouldn't care if she just fucked him. He'd fucked plenty of women without a second of remorse. But this was Stella, and he did care. He cared a whole fucking hell of a lot.

She fell into stride beside him. "Remember when I said I liked being dirty with you, but not with just any guy? Well, last night I wanted you to *fuck* me, because when you're inside me, it doesn't matter how dirty the words are, or how rough we are with each other. Everything we do feels different. It feels like…"

He stopped walking but didn't meet her gaze, afraid she'd see the hope in his eyes. Goddamn hope.

"I wasn't just fucking you, Logan. I was…"

He lifted his gaze at the softening of her tone just in time to see her crinkle her nose and look away, as if she were straining to find the right words.

"Love-fucking you," she spat.

"Love-fucking?" His shoulders lifted with a silent laugh.

She swatted his arm. "Yes. Love-fucking."

"What the hell is love-fucking? I think you just coined a new phrase."

"Love-fucking. You know. When you're falling for someone but you still want them to fuck you hard. *Love-fucking.*"

She crossed her arms, then nervously flung them straight again.

"So you're falling for me, but you don't want me to love you?" He had no idea what she was trying to say or how to respond.

"You can't love me, Logan. I'm just telling you that I wasn't fucking you. I was—"

He held up a hand, not wanting to hear it again. He'd felt the flicker of hope when she'd begun explaining, and now he was done. He narrowed his eyes and clenched his jaw to push his hopes away and regain perspective. He'd like to take her in his arms and kiss her until she realized that the heat that sparked every second they were together, and the lust that practically oozed from their skin when they kissed, was real. But he'd no sooner do that than allow himself to hope. He was done with hope. Hope was for losers, just like he'd told her. It was for weak people who couldn't change a damn thing and looked for some magical element to shift things into place.

This love stuff hurt like hell, and if he had to hope for her love, there was no way he was going to put himself through that sort of torture.

Then why did every ounce of him *hope* she was telling him the truth?

Chapter Sixteen

"DUDE, I DON'T know what you have going on with Stella, but if you're not going to hit that, I want a shot," Jackson said over Logan's shoulder.

Logan grabbed his younger brother's arm and squeezed his muscle. They were cooking spaghetti in his mother's kitchen. He and Stella had hardly spoken since she told him she'd love-fucked him. After a long, tense afternoon, and with the timeline on Kutcher's release closing in on them, Logan was in no mood for a pissing match over Stella. Logan eyed the entryway into the living room, where Stella and Heath were talking with his mother.

"Don't even think about it," Logan warned.

Jackson put his hands up in surrender. "Get a grip. What's gotten into you?"

Logan released him. "Sorry," he ground out. He knew Jackson was just messing around, but between waiting for the news on Kutcher and Stella pulsing hot and cold, Logan's nerves were threadbare.

Jackson lowered his voice. "Hey, man, I'd never make a move on your girl. I was just feeling you out."

"Not a good idea." He paced the small room. "She's got a lot of shit going on right now."

"She does, or you do?" Jackson held his stare.

"We both do." He stopped talking when Stella appeared in the doorway.

Her eyes darted between the two men. She fidgeted with the seam of her jeans. "Want some help?"

"Sure." Logan gave Jackson a stare that he knew he'd read as, *Get the hell out of here.*

Jackson pointed over his shoulder with his thumb. "I'll go talk with Mom."

Stella stood close enough that Logan could smell her fruity shampoo. "Your family's really nice."

"Thanks." He focused on stirring the spaghetti sauce, still trying to figure out how to handle things with her.

"Do you cook for your mom often?"

Logan shrugged. "We take turns throughout the week."

"*Every* week?"

He met her surprised gaze. "Yeah, well, since my father…"

Her eyes filled with empathy as she touched his arm. "I'm sorry, Logan."

Sorry for what? Breaking things off with me, or sorry about my mother? He wished he knew the answer.

"Yeah, well." He lifted a piece of spaghetti from the pot and plopped it into his mouth. It needed another minute.

"Your mom said the police gave up looking for the guy who broke in."

Logan shifted his eyes away, remembering the night he'd taken his parents' assailant's life and realizing that she wasn't sorry for breaking it off with him. He didn't want to talk about his father's death. He was having enough trouble trying to navigate their relationship. "Yup."

"Aren't you worried for her with him still out there?"

Logan hadn't told his mother that he'd killed her attacker,

but she'd believed Logan when he'd told her the guy had been taken care of. He didn't know what his mother thought that meant, and he had no desire to find out. She was safe, and that was all that mattered. As for Stella, he was done pussyfooting around. He was no better at feigning his emotions than she was at it, no matter how hard she tried to play it cool.

He slid his hand around her waist, ignoring the way her body tensed against his.

"I don't want to talk about my father." He held her gaze. "Stella, you can resist me, but I'm here, and I'm not going anywhere."

"Logan." She turned away and lowered her voice. "You don't need someone like me in your life. You have a great family, a great life, and I have Kutcher."

He turned her in his arms again and touched her cheek, guiding her eyes back to his. "I want *you*, and I feel like you want me, too, but you're fighting it."

"Am not."

He smiled at the adorable way she said the lie. "You can fool yourself, sweetheart, but you're not fooling me."

"You see what you want to see," she snapped, but her body belied her tone. Her hips pressed into his. He splayed his hands across her lower back and noticed the pulse at the base of her neck quickening.

"I like what I see, but I don't see how you feel about me," he said. "I feel it."

She rolled her eyes, but Logan refused to be dissuaded. This love was real; he'd bet his life on it. He pressed a kiss to her cheek and whispered, "You feel it, too, darlin', and I'll be right here waiting when you can no longer fight it."

Heath appeared in the doorway, and Stella quickly disengaged from his arms with a look of a guilty teenager caught necking on the couch.

"Sorry to interrupt. Just thought I'd grab the plates." Heath reached into a cabinet.

Logan enjoyed watching Stella squirm. She looked cute as hell, all pink-cheeked and flustered.

"Thanks, Heath." Logan arched a brow at Stella, who widened her eyes as if to say, *Now look what you did.*

He drained and rinsed the pasta and coughed to muffle a chuckle.

As soon as Heath left the room, she whispered, "Stop touching me."

"Okay." He shrugged like it was no big deal and transferred the pasta into a bowl, then poured the sauce into another serving dish.

"I mean it," she snapped.

"I said, okay."

The back door swung open and Cooper sauntered in. "Logan, my man." He pulled Logan into a manly embrace, which included a hard slap on the back, then zeroed in on Stella. "Well, well, well. Who is this?" He extended a hand, turning on his Wild charm. "Hi. I'm Cooper."

"Hi, I'm St-Stella."

Logan glanced over at her hesitation. Had she been about to say Stormy out of habit, or was she momentarily caught in his brother's midnight-blue eyes?

Cooper lifted her hand to his lips and kissed the back of it. "You should let me shoot you sometime. You have great features."

"Down, boy," Logan teased. "Coop's a photographer. He and Jackson own a photography studio."

"I could make you a star." Cooper raked an appraising eye down her body, and Logan picked up on her discomfort.

"Coop," Logan warned with a narrow-eyed stare.

"Sorry. Industry hazard." Cooper ran his eyes between them. "So, you're with Logan?"

Logan said, "Yes," at the same time Stella said, "Sort of."

"She's here with me, Coop." He shook his head, refusing to be dissuaded. "The jury's still out on what *with* means."

"Got it. Thanks for cooking. Need me to grab anything? Forks? Glasses?"

"Nah, we've got it covered. Thanks."

"Cool. Where's Mom?" Cooper followed Logan's nod toward the living room.

"It's like I walked into a *GQ* fashion shoot," Stella said quietly.

"Coop's pretty handsome," Logan admitted.

"Oh, please. Like you don't know you're even better-looking than him?" Stella lifted her chin with the challenge.

"Doesn't matter what I think. It's what you think that matters." He handed her the sauce dish.

"I think I'm damn lucky to be having dinner with four handsome men, but it's really kind of unfair. Four tall, dark, and blue-eyed brothers, with rock-hard bodies built for a fight? Seriously. What did your parents do, pay off the DNA police?"

Logan laughed and picked up the bowl of spaghetti. He leaned in close and whispered, "I may be built for a fight, but I think you know my body's made for lovin'."

IF STELLA HADN'T known that Mary Lou Wild was blind,

she might not have noticed when they'd first arrived that Logan's mother couldn't see. Within a few seconds of their arrival in her living room, where she had been sitting in a recliner and knitting, Mary Lou had set her knitting needles aside and risen to her feet. She'd looked directly at Logan and opened her arms. *Lovey*, she'd said. Before Logan had a chance to introduce Stella, his mother had turned in her direction and smiled, as if she had sensed Stella standing beside him. She reached a hand out and drew Stella into an equally warm embrace, tugging at Stella's ache for her own mother's touch.

Stella watched her now as she ate dinner as if she weren't blind. She seemed to sense where things were on her plate and never once fished for her glass on the table.

His mother folded her napkin and set it on the table beside her plate. "Lovey, dinner was delicious."

Stella sat between Logan and Mary Lou, across from his brothers, Heath, Cooper, and Jackson. Sitting at a real dinner table with a real family again brought down more of Stella's defenses. Logan's knee kept brushing hers, and he'd draped an arm over the back of her chair. Her body pleaded for her to lean in to him, to give in to what they both wanted, but she was still afraid of what tomorrow would bring.

"You always have to outdo me," Coop teased.

"That's not hard to do. You never actually cook." Logan turned his attention to Stella. "Coop's idea of cooking dinner for the family is bringing takeout with him instead of having it delivered."

Cooper pointed his fork at Logan. "Hey, I made burgers over the summer."

"It's true. He brought the premade patties and everything," Heath teased.

"Look who's talking," Jackson countered. "Last week you brought frozen lasagna."

"Boys, that's enough bickering." Every word Mary Lou spoke was layered in love for her children, and it brought Stella's longing for her mother closer to the surface. "I'm thankful that you have dinner with me at all. You all have successful careers and you're so busy." She shook her head. "Stella, do you know that there isn't a night of the week that one of my boys isn't here with me? Not a single night, bless their hearts. They think I'm an invalid."

"We do not," Logan and Jackson said in unison.

"It's our pleasure, Mom." Heath reached across the table and touched his mother's hand. "We're lucky that you make time for us."

"Oh, honey. Please." She leaned toward Stella again. "Luckiest mother around, I tell you."

Stella felt her throat thickening. What she wouldn't give to have dinner with her mother. Just one night. Maybe now that Logan had figured out how Kutcher was tracking her, she'd be able to go see her without Kutcher knowing.

Maybe hope wasn't such a bad thing after all.

"Good to hear your shoot went well today," Logan said.

Stella wondered if he'd sensed her need to change the subject. He'd been checking in with her all evening. Making sure she was okay. It would be easier to ignore her feelings for him if he weren't so attentive and caring.

Holy crap.

What am I doing? I don't want to ignore my feelings. I want Logan—without Kutcher breathing down our backs.

"We're shooting the teasers for a movie your friend Zane Walker's in in a few weeks," Cooper said to Logan. "You should come watch. It'll be fun. We're shooting in Sweetwater, by your cabin."

"Really? Maybe we will," Logan answered.

We?

The smile Logan flashed told her that he'd meant to use the word *we*, and it made her heart tumble in her chest. Darn heart. She was supposed to be keeping her distance, but it was hard to do around him, and being near his family made it even more difficult. They were warm and friendly, and she loved the way they teased one another. She'd often wished for siblings when she was growing up, and she imagined if she'd had them, they would have been as close-knit as Logan's family. Maybe a few savvy older brothers would have warned her away from Kutcher in the first place.

"Logan said you met Willow," Jackson said. "Did she make you her famous cupcakes?"

"The pink-frosted ones?" she asked, remembering the sweet deliciousness. "Yes, and they were delicious. It's a good thing I don't work with her all the time. I'd weigh three hundred pounds."

"You'd be the sexiest three-hundred-pound woman on earth," Logan said.

She touched his thigh, realizing too late that instinct had taken action before she'd had a chance to stop it. His hand came down on hers and held on tight.

"He's such a flirt," Mary Lou said.

"Yes. He doesn't know when to quit." Stella tried to give Logan a serious stare, but she knew she'd failed because it was hard to look harsh around a man who was looking at her like she really was the most beautiful woman on earth.

"Oh, lovey," Mary Lou said quietly. "He's not going to

quit. These boys don't have any control over their hearts. Neither do you, sweetie." She moved her head as if she were looking around the table at each of her sons. Heath's, Jackson's, and Cooper's brows were furrowed with disbelief. Logan was grinning like a Cheshire cat. "Your heart knows its mate before you're even aware something's going on, and when it figures out who that person is, you're about as powerful as a feather in the wind. There's nothing you can do but go along for the ride."

Jackson scoffed. "Well, I'm doing just fine without taking that particular ride."

"Of course you are, Jackson." Mary Lou turned toward Jackson's voice. "Your heart's still untethered, but Logan…"

"Mom," Logan warned.

"Lovey, I'm not telling tales. Your hearts are tethered. A mother knows these things."

Stella's jaw dropped open at his mother's candor.

Mary Lou patted Stella's arm. "Close your mouth, dear."

Stella was entranced by the way Mary Lou picked up on things most sighted people wouldn't notice.

"Did you have any more trouble with that guy at the bar?" Heath asked.

"No. Thanks to Logan." She glanced at Logan. She'd never thought to ask him how he'd known the guy had dragged her into the alley the other night. Or why he'd been following them in the first place. It seemed like he'd been placed in her life when she needed him most. Her guardian angel. And he hadn't tried to get away from her once. Any other man would have been long gone.

But not Logan.

He'd made a promise that first night to keep her safe.

He was committed.

He was in love.

With me.

Mary Lou leaned closer to Stella and said quietly, "He's a good man."

"Mom, I don't need any pimping," Logan said.

"We all need pimping now and again, Logan," his mother said. "Besides, I'm not telling her anything she doesn't already know."

She was right, even if Stella was trying to ignore the way he fawned over her, checking to see if she needed more wine or wanted more spaghetti. Or the way he'd taken her to his cabin. Even his leaving her with Willow was done out of love.

I'm hoping to give you a few hours of remembering what it was like to live without watching your back.

"I heard you're working for Dylan," Jackson said, pulling her back to the conversation.

"Yes, for now."

"For now? Do you hope to do something else?" Jackson glanced at Logan.

Hope? No, she knew better than to hope. "Not really. Before I moved I worked as an interior designer. I really enjoyed it."

"Interior design? Jackson, we could use her at the studio as a stager, can't we? I mean, if you want to get out of the bartending business," Cooper offered.

She glanced at Logan, who shrugged and smiled his approval. She was afraid to get excited. They were very high-profile photographers, which would surely lead Kutcher right to her.

"That's really nice of you, but..." *I'm not sure if I'll have to leave town again, or if I'll live for another week, or—*

Logan draped an arm over her shoulder. "Thanks, Coop. She's got a lot going on right now, but she may take you up on that offer in the future."

"Interior design, that's something I've always been interested in," Mary Lou said. "Tell us about your family, Stella. Do you have any siblings?"

Stella had thought she'd escaped personal questions, since no one had asked her until now. She wondered if Logan had filled them all in on her situation, but apparently not. She was glad he hadn't breached her confidence. Logan shifted his eyes to her and opened his mouth to say something, but just as he started to respond, his cell phone rang.

"Excuse me." He withdrew his phone from his pocket and rose to his feet. He walked into the living room, and a minute later Stella heard the front door open and close.

Her stomach took a nosedive.

"Honey, you're putting off some very nervous energy. Are you okay?" Mary Lou asked.

No, I'm not okay. I want to run after him and find out if the call is about Kutcher. All eyes were on her as she fidgeted in her seat.

"Yes, I'm fine."

A minute later the front door opened and Logan strode into the dining room with a stern set jaw and a sheen of determination in his eyes.

"I'm sorry, Ma, but we have to take off." Logan reached for Stella's hand.

"What? Why?" his mother asked.

"Logan, anything we can help with?" Heath was on his feet in the blink of an eye, as were Jackson and Cooper.

Logan was already on the move, with one hand on Stella's lower back, guiding her out the door, the other hand firmly around her upper arm. His brothers were right behind them.

"I've got this. Take care of Mom."

Chapter Seventeen

"WHAT IS GOING on?" Stella asked as he helped her into the car. "Logan, please. Just tell me what's going on."

She had begun trembling the minute he'd taken her hand, and now the color had drained from her face. The call from the police had brought the best and the worst news. He hated that she'd have to face Kutcher again, but it was the only way to ensure that the dirtbag stayed behind bars for the longest possible time.

He climbed into the driver's seat and started the car. "We have to go to Mystic."

"Mystic?" Her voice cracked.

She reached for his hand.

She *trusted* him.

"Kanets talked, so Kutcher is being held. He can't get out tomorrow, Stella. They'll detain him and with a new trial, his sentence will likely be extended by several years."

"So why do we have to go there?" Her voice shook as badly as her hand.

He kept his eyes on the road as he followed the ramp onto the busy highway.

"The only way to keep him behind bars for long enough to make a difference is for you to identify him as your assailant from the knife attack."

She pulled her hand from his and moved closer to the passenger door. "No. No, Logan. I can't do that. I won't do that."

"Why, Stella? Do you want to worry about him getting out in three years? Five years?" He reached for her hand, and she turned away. "Stella, if he's in jail, he can't hurt you. If you don't do this, you'll be afraid forever."

Tears sprang from her eyes. "I don't want to see him. I can't. Logan, I can't do this."

"Stella—"

"No. I don't want to see..." Sobs strangled her voice. "I can't look at him."

He pulled off at the next exit and drove into a parking lot.

"Please, Logan, don't make me see him." He came around to her side of the car, crouched beside her, and pulled her into his arms, holding her against him as sobs racked her body. He'd known he was taking a chance when he spoke to the police and turned in her phone and the bug he'd found in her picture frame. He'd known she'd hate the idea of identifying Kutcher to the police, but it was the only way to keep her safe.

"I know this is hard, Stella, but you can put him away for twenty years. Twenty years, baby. You can live your life, have a future without a fake name, without looking over your shoulder. You can see your mother."

She fisted her hands in his shirt, burying her face in his chest. "I can't."

He appealed to her heart instead of her head. "Do you want him to go free and potentially hurt someone else?"

She held her breath.

"Breathe, baby. I've got you. Breathe. In and out."

She let out a breath and hitched in another one.

"That's it. That's my girl." He stroked her back, her head,

held her tightly against him. He would breathe for her if he could. He knew how terrible facing Kutcher would be, but it was the only way.

"I'll be right there with you, and he won't be able to see you when you identify him."

"But he'll know. *I* was the one he attacked."

Logan drew back and gazed into her damp, puffy eyes. "Baby, he can't hurt you anymore. There are no more bugs. He can't find you or bother you anymore. He's going to stay behind bars for a long time, and you have the power to make that even longer. I will be right there with you."

"But I've been awful to you."

"No, baby. You've been afraid. You're the strongest woman I know, and even if you don't love me, I'll always be there to protect you."

Fresh sobs bubbled from her chest. "But I do. I do love you. I'm just so tired of being afraid, Logan, and I'm so scared all the time."

"You don't have to say that, Stormy." The name slid from his lips like an endearment. She would always be *his* Stormy. "Don't say what you don't mean."

"Logan, I do love you. God, you know I do. I fell for you the night we met, but I'm scared. Scared of losing you. Scared of being attacked. Scared of ruining your life because of Kutcher."

He pulled her in close again, soaking in her words. "I know you are, but I'm here, and I'm not going anywhere. You'll never be alone again." He felt her fingers dig into his skin as she fisted her hands in the back of his shirt, and he knew she was readying herself for something.

"Logan?" She looked directly into his eyes.

"Yes, darlin'?"

"I'll do it. Kutcher's taken enough of my life already. I'm not willing to let him take you away from me, too."

Chapter Eighteen

IT HAD BEEN a long time since Stella had lived without fear, and at three o'clock in the morning, after filing the report and identifying Kutcher as her attacker, she took what felt like her first real breath in six months. A hazy glow surrounded the moon in the starless sky, barely illuminating the parking lot of the Mystic hotel. Stella had spent six months attuned to her surroundings. Six long months waiting to be attacked, sleeping with one eye and one ear open. She'd spent almost as long doing everything she could to separate herself from anything linking back to her mother. Now, thanks to the man who was opening the passenger door and reaching for her hand—the man who said he'd take care of her from the moment he'd rescued her from the guy in the alley and had proven it every minute since—she would get to see her mother in a few short hours.

She took Logan's hand and walked silently into the brightly lit and elegant hotel lobby. The receptionist smiled up at them, her eyes lingering on Logan with appreciation and interest. Logan draped an arm over Stella's shoulder and kissed her temple.

"We'd like your best suite, please," Logan said.

"Yes, sir, and the name?" The pretty blonde fluttered her lashes flirtatiously.

Stella gazed into Logan's eyes, lifted her chin, and for the first time in what felt like forever, proudly gave her name.

"Krane. Stella Krane."

The suite was enormous, decorated with warm hues and boasting a view of the harbor. Stella stood at the balcony, thinking about how much her life had changed since Logan had come into it and anticipating seeing her mother tomorrow. She wished they could have made the ten-minute drive tonight, but it would only frighten her mother to have someone come to her door at such an early hour. Besides, she was sure she looked as tired as she felt. Logan's arms circled her waist from behind. He pressed his cheek to hers, and she nestled against his chest.

"Isn't it beautiful?" she whispered.

"Yes. You are."

She reached up and touched his stubbly cheek, then turned in his arms. His eyes were warm, his embrace strong, and she knew she was right where she was supposed to be, but now that she knew that Kutcher would likely be out of the picture for many years, she allowed herself to want, and dream, and hope.

"I want to get to know you better, Logan."

"Darlin', you know me pretty damn well. You've even met my family." He kissed her forehead.

"I want to know all of you. I want to know why you didn't answer me about being scared for your mom, knowing your father's killer is still out there."

"That's a lot of getting to know me." Logan smiled, but it wasn't a tense smile. He seemed okay with her request. "You may not like what you hear."

"A very wise man told me that we couldn't erase the past. You accepted my past without question. Your love and trust in me never wavered. I want you to know that whatever happened in your past, I accept it. I want to be part of your future, too."

"You may change your mind."

"No. I have faith in you. No matter what you tell me, I know that whatever happened in your past happened because it had to. Because you felt it was the right thing to do at the time, no matter what it was."

He touched his forehead to hers and whispered, "I hope you mean that."

"With all my heart." She went up on her toes, twined her arms around his neck, and pressed her mouth to his. "Make love to me. I need you."

"Stella." A plea. "I want you more than I want to breathe, but if I make love to you and *then* tell you about my past and you decide to leave…" He looked away for a beat, his eyes awash with worry. "I thought I lost you for good last night. I can't go through that again."

He took her hand and led her inside to the couch.

"I'm not going to leave." She couldn't imagine being more in love with any man, but after the way she'd vacillated and what she'd put them through, she understood his hesitation. "I know I hurt you, and I hurt myself. You have no reason to trust my word, Logan. But I'm not going anywhere."

"I trust your word. But what you think of me right now might change, no matter how good your intentions are." He touched her cheek, and the side of his mouth quirked up in a pained smile.

He proceeded to tell her about his time with the SEALs, the number of people he'd killed, and what it had felt like when he'd looked into the enemies' eyes and taken them down. He spoke with vehemence and passion, stopping several times to gather his thoughts or his courage—she wasn't sure which. And then he sat quietly for a long while, gazing at their linked hands.

"Are you still with me?" he asked tentatively.

She moved closer to him, their thighs pressed against each other, hips touching. "More so than ever."

He nodded, as if that pleased him, though his facial expression remained serious.

"What my mother told you was true. The police stopped searching for the man who blinded my mother and killed my father." He pressed his finger and thumb to his eyes.

"You don't have to continue."

He nodded. "Yes. Yes, I do. If you think you want to make a life with me, you need to know."

The torment in his voice nearly slayed her. "Okay," she whispered.

"I was on a mission when my parents were attacked. I'll never forgive myself for not being here. I know I might not have been around to save them, but that guilt will never leave—you need to understand that. It will always be a part of me, driving me in everything I do."

"Okay."

He nodded again, furrowing his brow. "I ran my own investigation and I found clues the police missed, but they dismissed me. I don't blame them. I was off the wall, Stella. I wasn't the man I am now. I lost my mind when my father died and my mom..." His eyes welled with tears and he turned away. "When Mom was..."

"Logan."

His hands fisted. "I stormed into the precinct, demanding I don't even know what. Justice, I guess. They saw me as a crazed son, distraught, out of my mind." He stared straight ahead.

"I took it into my own hands. Talked to everyone I could,

lived in the pawn shops until my dad's family ring showed up. It was an antique, worth only a few hundred bucks. Waste of a life. I tracked the guy down who did it and went to the police, but they said there wasn't enough evidence. My mom couldn't identify him."

"Oh, Logan."

"I followed him. Guys like that, they have an MO and they don't change much. I caught him casing a house, went back to the police again, but they ignored me, so…" He shook his head. "One night when I was tailing him, he broke into a house. Single mother, two-year-old son." He gritted his teeth. "I called the police, and I waited. I waited, Stella. I wait—" He looked away again with pain-filled eyes.

An ache of foreboding clung to her. "Logan, you don't have to fill me in on the rest."

"I do. By the time I got inside, he had a knife to the woman's throat. She looked right at me. Crying, begging me to help her. Her kid was screaming in the other room, and I didn't think. I just reacted."

Stella held her breath, struggling to remain focused around the obvious pain and guilt pulling Logan under.

"When I dragged him away from her, he slit her neck." Logan's voice cracked. "He had a gun in his waistband."

She remembered the white trail that led down his body to a scar on his stomach. "Your scars."

"Knife, bullet. I didn't feel either. I heard that baby crying, saw the woman bleeding, and I attacked. I turned off all senses and just…" Logan clenched his eyes and mouth shut. He pressed both hands to the sides of his head, as if he could squeeze the memory from it, and bowed his head.

"I killed the motherfucker. I don't know if the police came

because of my phone call or if neighbors heard the attack. But they dragged me from his limp body."

"The woman?"

He nodded. "She needed thirty stitches, but she survived. She moved away shortly after that. I killed him, Stella."

"You were stabbed and shot." He'd saved them both even with life-threatening wounds. Thoughts filtered through her mind, but she was too stunned to speak. *Committed. Strong. Logan.*

"I killed the bastard, and they found this in his wallet." He pulled out his wallet and showed her his father's ID card from the factory where he'd worked.

"But your mother?"

"She doesn't know I killed him. She just knows that she's safe." Logan scrubbed his hand down his face. When he lifted his eyes to hers, a tear slipped down her cheek. Logan reached up and wiped it away with his thumb. "I'm sorry, darlin'. It's too much. That's why I wanted to tell you before we ended up in bed together."

She pressed his hand to her cheek. "No, Logan. It's not too much. I think I love you more than I did before you told me."

That night when their bodies joined together, their love felt new and different. She saw heartrending tenderness in Logan's gaze as he studied her, loved her, his hands playing over her body as if he were memorizing all of her. His touch made her senses spin and her body ache for more. She was extremely conscious of his virility and his sensuality. Roughness was replaced with soothing passion, and words like *fuck* were obliterated from her mind by warmer, more loving thoughts.

"I want to cherish you, adore you. I want to taste every inch of your silky skin," he whispered as he studied the dips and curves of her body.

His appreciative gaze roved over her, followed by his mouth, his tongue, his talented fingers. He shifted, gently tucking her curves beneath his firm, muscular frame, and finally—*God, finally*—he slid inside her. Their bodies moved in perfect harmony, stoking the flames burning within her, deepening and intensifying their love. He filled her completely with every loving word, every passionate kiss, every thrust of his powerful hips, shattering her last shred of control and taking them into a sea of pure, explosive pleasure.

Chapter Nineteen

LOGAN HELPED STELLA from the car. She'd hardly said two words on the drive from the hotel to her mother's house. A deep vee had formed between her brows when they left the hotel, and it had been there ever since. She had a death grip on his hand.

"What's wrong?"

"I…" She turned worried eyes up to him. "Are you sure Kutcher isn't going to get out?"

Logan knew this fear would be with her for a very long time. "Yes. He'll have to go through the legal process to get a conviction, but this is a sealed deal. He's going to be behind bars for a long time. You've given them a positive identification on Kutcher. They're talking to the neighbor who interrupted the attack to get an ID from him, too. They have the physical evidence they need to convict him. They had the DNA samples from the hospital visit after he stabbed you. He's done, darlin', and I'll be with you every step of the way." They'd been over this a dozen times that morning, and Logan was ready to reassure her a dozen more. Whatever it took, he was in, one hundred percent.

Stella breathed deeply as they waited for her mother to answer the door. They heard shuffling, and a voice similar to Stella's called through the closed door, "Who is it?"

Tears sprang from Stella's eyes. "It's me, Mom. It's Stella."

They listened to two bolts sliding free, and the door opened as far as the chain lock would allow. A set of tired green eyes peered out at them, instantly filling with tears as they darted between Stella and Logan.

"It's really me, Mom. It's okay. It's safe."

A moment later Stella was wrapped in her mother's arms, both of them crying, and Logan's heart felt as if it had doubled in size. He turned away to give them privacy. Still within her mother's embrace, Stella snagged his shirt.

"Stay."

He did.

He always would.

Her mother's cancer was in remission. Her hair had begun growing back, and although she appeared thin and tired, by the time they left several hours later, both Stella and her mother looked as if new life had been breathed into them. Stella had a bounce to her step, and Logan swore her eyes looked brighter than ever.

Stella stood beside the car, looking at her mother's house for a long while. When she was ready, Logan opened the car door so they could leave.

She wrapped her arms around his waist and pressed her cheek to his chest.

"Thank you for everything, Logan. You've done too much for me already, but there's something else I'd like you to do."

"Anything, darlin'. You know that."

"We can't escape our pasts, but we can be free from them and put them behind us."

"That's what we're doing."

"No," she said. "That's what I'm doing. Now it's your turn.

I wish you would come clean to your mother, let her know what happened so that you can put that burden behind you."

A chill ran through him at the prospect. Logan shook his head. "I don't want my mother thinking of me as a cold-blooded killer. This is different."

"What you did wasn't cold-blooded, Logan. You saved that woman and her son. You probably saved many women that night. Your mother will be proud of you. She deserves to know as much as you deserve to be relieved of the guilt that you've been carrying around for so long. I love you, but I can't see how we can move forward with that noose hanging around your neck."

Logan had thought about telling his mother a million times, and the thought had nearly suffocated him. It was one thing to handle a mission for his country. He could disconnect from the emotions when he was carrying out a duty to protect his country, but this…This was his personal mission. No one hired him to do it. All he could imagine was his mother thinking about him killing that man with his bare hands.

"Please?" Stella stepped in closer. "For us? At least think about it?"

One look with her penetrating, love-filled gaze, and he fell under her spell, just as he'd been since the day he met her. He'd give his life for Stella if he had to. But this. This was the toughest thing he'd ever been asked to do. And for Stella, he'd do anything.

Earning Stella's trust and love had changed him. She'd become *his* last night, and he'd been hers since the moment he'd followed her into that alley and rescued her.

He just hadn't known that he'd needed rescuing, too.

Now Available
WILD BOYS AFTER DARK: HEATH

No last names. No strings. No ties.
Except of the silk variety.

Dr. Heath Wild and Allyson Jenner only wanted a simple tryst. But Heath couldn't live with just one night, just one taste, of Ally—and Ally couldn't escape the memory of his hands on her skin, the way he looked at her like she was his obsession, or his seduction, which had pushed her to the edge and had made her want to do things she never had before.

One night leads to one tantalizing phone call. Can one phone call lead to forever?

Chapter One

FUCKING PERFECT. THOSE words played over and over in Dr. Heath Wild's mind as he thrust his tongue deeper into the receptive mouth of the sexy woman who was grinding her hips against his cock in the elevator of the Gray Mountain Lodge. He buried his hands in her hair and gave a less-than-gentle tug, testing the woman's boundaries. The sexy moan that followed was all the green light he needed to press her up against the wall and pin her wrists above her head with one large, capable hand, while thrusting his other beneath her little black dress and into her—*thong, hot damn*—beneath. He didn't waste any time finding his way inside this beautiful, willing creature. Her head tipped back, and he claimed her neck, sucking as he fingered her hot, wet center.

"Oh God. Yes. Right there," she panted.

Acutely aware that the elevator was about to reach the sixth floor, he circled his thumb over her swollen clit as he claimed her mouth in another ravishing kiss. She clawed at his dress shirt, making sounds that had him picturing her spread-eagle on his bed, arms restrained, with his face buried between her legs.

"Ah. Fuck." She dug her hands into his thick hair as the orgasm gripped her—and the elevator chimed.

Heath casually fixed her dress, unhurried by the elevator doors sliding open. He drank in her flushed cheeks, the light sheen of sweat on her upper lip that he wanted to lick off, and her full, heaving breasts.

"Open your eyes, sweetheart," he said in a gravelly voice. He wanted more, and he was about to get it.

ALLYSON JENNER TRIED to act nonchalant as she passed an elderly couple in the hallway on the way to her room, hoping they didn't smell sex wafting around her and the incredibly hot guy she was with. She lifted her chin as she unlocked the door, acting as if her hands weren't shaking, like she did this type of thing every day, as the mind-blowing kisser she was about to fuck obviously did. She might not do it every day, but she wasn't a stranger to hooking up with random guys, either. She enjoyed sex the way others might enjoy an occasional swim in the ocean; reveling in the shocking experience at first, then giving in to the exquisite pleasures, and finally, when she was satiated, going back to her normal life feeling rejuvenated for the next few months.

The door clicked shut, and the sound of the dead bolt sliding into place brought her back to the handsome man licking his lips. His piercing blue eyes raked over her body, lingering on her breasts. The edges of his mouth quirked up as he loosened his tie and cracked his neck to either side. Her nerves prickled. This was the moment she had to push past—the urge to flee from fear of the unknown. What if he was a psychopath? What if the staff found her bloodied body in the bathroom tomorrow morning? She'd watched him all afternoon at the medical conference downstairs. She hadn't missed that, while she'd been sizing him up, he'd been stalking her like prey, and it had turned her on before he'd even bought her a drink after the conference. She really should have gotten his name. What had she been thinking?

She knew exactly what she'd been thinking, because the thought had only grown more intense with every passing minute. She wanted to feel his powerful body above her, his arms around her, and the enormous cock bulging beneath his zipper and outlined by his dress pants inside her.

He clutched her hips and tugged her against his expensive suit, taking her in another mind-numbing kiss. She fumbled with the buttons on his shirt, desperate to get to the smattering of chest hair she'd seen peeking out of the top. She could feel the strength of him in his kiss, in his grip, in the rock wall behind her hands. He was easily six two or six three. She was five five, maybe five eight in her heels, and he—*what's his name?*—still had several inches on her.

"What's your name?" she asked between kisses.

"Heath."

Heath. She liked that. Smooth and hot, like him. She'd always loved a man's man. A man who made her feel feminine but didn't treat her like she was a delicate flower. A man who took what he wanted but still made her feel special, and this guy had stroked her hand when they were in the bar, not her thigh. His eyes read, *I'm going to fuck you hard,* but his actions told her he knew how to respect *and* pleasure a woman. Crazy, she knew, because how much could he respect a stranger he was about to fuck? But if he'd put his hand on her thigh in public, it would have sent a completely different message.

"Ally," she offered.

The edges of his mouth curled up, but his eyes turned midnight dark as he tore her dress over her head, tossed it on the chair, and pulled her against him again.

"I cannot wait to get my mouth on you, *Ally*. To taste your come and feel you shatter against my tongue."

Her insides caught fire. If he could make her come with his fingers in less than a minute, she could only imagine what he could do with that viperous tongue of his.

Breathe, Ally. Be patient.

He rubbed the pad of his thumb over her bottom lip and ground his hips against hers, sending *patient* out the window.

"I want to feel your luscious lips wrapped around my cock."

His voice was liquid lust, and it was all she could do to whisper, "Yes."

She clawed at his shirt, the button of his trousers, his tie, desperate for him to fulfill his promise. He grabbed her wrists and trapped them by her hips.

"You in a hurry?" He lowered his mouth to her neck and sucked.

Yes. I want you inside me. "No." She squeezed her thighs together to try to satiate the longing between her legs. Every suck and stroke of his tongue made her nipples harder—if that was even possible. Good Lord, he was going to make her come without even touching her below the waist.

He stepped back, assessing her body with those lust-filled eyes again, pinning her in place as they slowly dragged over her.

"You're fucking beautiful, *Ally*." Her name slid off his tongue like a sensual promise. He took his time stripping off his trousers and dress shirt, leaving his tie loose around his neck and his black Calvin Klein boxer briefs covering his enormous erection.

Heat thrummed through her at his casual striptease.

"Heath what?" The question was driven by nerves.

His confidence was titillating, the way he languidly laid his dress shirt over the back of the chair, then did the same with his pants. He stopped mid-move, pulled his shoulders back, and eyed her skeptically. In the space of a breath, Ally drank in his five-o'clock shadow, which gave him an edgy aura. His skin pulled taut over his handsome, squarish face and strong jaw. He had full lips, and his mouth was slightly small—though she already knew it gave great pleasure. He turned, squaring his broad shoulders, and her eyes dipped south, to the perfect planes of flesh before her.

"I'm not looking for anything more than tonight, Ally. No last names, no talk of what we do for a living. Just a night of intense pleasure. Are you okay with that?" He lowered his chin, and his eyes implored her to answer.

"Yes," she said with confidence. That's what she'd been assuming anyway. Nothing new there, but hearing the words made her feel a little...something. *Cheap?* No. Definitely not. They brought a rush that was even more powerful, more enjoyable.

To continue reading, buy
WILD BOYS AFTER DARK: HEATH

Please enjoy a preview of another
Love in Bloom novel

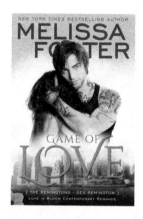

Ellie Parker is a master at building walls around her heart. In the twenty-five years she's been alive, Dex Remington has been the only person who has always believed in her and been there for her. But four years earlier, she came to Dex seeking comfort and then disappeared like a thief in the night, leaving him a broken man.

Dex Remington is one of the top PC game developers in the United States. He's handsome, smart, and numb. So damn numb that he's not sure he'll ever find a reason to feel again.

A chance encounter sparks intense desires in Ellie and Dex. Desires that make her want to run—and make him want to feel. A combination of lust and fear leads these young lovers down a dangerous path. Is it possible to cross a burned bridge, or are they destined to be apart forever?

Chapter One

DEX REMINGTON WALKED into NightCaps bar beside his older brother Sage, an artist who also lived in New York City, and Regina Smith, his employee and right arm. Women turned in their direction as they came through the door, their hungry eyes raking over Dex's and Sage's wide shoulders and muscular physiques. At six foot four, Sage had two inches on Dex, and with their striking features, dark hair, and federal-blue eyes, heads spun everywhere they went. But after Dex had worked thirty of the last forty-eight hours, women were the furthest thing from his mind. His four-star-general father had ingrained hard work and dedication into his head since he was old enough to walk, and no matter how much he rued his father's harsh parenting, following his lead had paid off. At twenty-six, Dex was one of the country's leading PC game designers and the founder of Thrive Entertainment, a multimillion-dollar gaming corporation. His father had taught him another valuable lesson—how to become numb—making it easy for him to disconnect from the women other men might find too alluring to ignore.

Dex was a stellar student. He'd been numb for a very long time.

"Thanks for squeezing in a quick beer with me," he said to Sage. They had about twenty minutes to catch up before his scheduled meeting with Regina and Mitch Anziano, another of his Thrive employees. They were going to discuss the game they were rolling out in three weeks, *World of Thieves II*.

"You're kidding, right? I should be saying that to you." Sage threw his arm around Dex's shoulder. They had an ongoing rivalry about who was the busiest, and with Sage's travel and gallery schedule and Dex working all night and getting up midday, it was tough to pick a winner.

"Thrive!" Mitch hollered from the bar in his usual greeting. Mitch used *Thrive!* to greet Dex in bars the way others used, *Hey.* He lifted his glass, and a smile spread across his unshaven cheeks. At just over five foot eight with three days' beard growth trailing down his neck like fur and a gut that he was all too proud of, he was what the world probably thought all game designers looked like. And worth his weight in gold. Mitch could outprogram anyone, and he was more loyal than a golden retriever.

Regina lifted her chin and elbowed Dex. "He's early." She slinked through the crowded bar, pulling Dex along behind her. Her Levi's hung low, cinched across her protruding hip bones by a studded black leather belt. Her red hoodie slipped off one shoulder, exposing the colorful tattoos that ran across her shoulder and down her arms.

Mitch and Regina had been Dex's first employees when he'd opened his company. Regina handled the administrative aspects of the company, kept the production schedule, monitored the program testing, and basically made sure nothing slipped through the cracks, while Mitch, like Dex, conceptually and technically designed games with the help of the rest of Thrive's fifty employees—developers, testers, and a host of programmers and marketing specialists.

Regina climbed onto the barstool beside Mitch and lifted his beer to her lips.

"Order ours yet?" she asked with a glint in her heavily lined dark eyes. She ran her hand through her stick-straight, jet-black hair.

Dex climbed onto the stool beside her as the bartender slid beers in front of him and Regina. "Thanks, Jon. Got a brew for my brother?"

"Whatever's on tap," Sage said. "Hey, Mitch. Good to see you."

Mitch lifted his beer with a nod of acknowledgment.

Dex took a swig of the cold ale, closed his eyes, and sighed, savoring the taste.

"Easy, big boy. We need you sober if you wanna win a GOTY." Mitch took a sip of Regina's beer. "Fair's fair."

Regina rolled her eyes and reached a willowy arm behind him, then mussed his mop of curly dark hair. "We're gonna win Game of the Year no matter what. Reviewers love us. Right, Dex?"

Thrive had already produced three games, one of which, *World of Thieves*, had made Dex a major player in the gaming world—and earned him millions of dollars. His biggest competitor, KI Industries, had changed the release date for their new game. KI would announce the new date publicly at midnight, and since their game was supposed to be just as hot of a game as they expected *World of Thieves II* to be, if they released close to the release for *World of Thieves II*, there would be a clear winner and a clear loser. Dex had worked too hard to be the loser.

"That's the hope," Dex said. He took another swig of his beer and checked his watch. Eight forty-five and his body thought it was noon. He'd spent so many years working all night and sleeping late that his body clock was completely thrown off. He was ready for a big meal and the start of his workday. He stroked the stubble along his chin. "I worked on it till four this morning. I think I deserve a cold one."

Sage leaned in to him. "You're not nervous about the release, are you?"

Of his five siblings—including Dex's twin sister, Siena, Sage knew him best. He was the quintessential artist, with a heart that outweighed the millions of dollars his sculptures had earned him. He'd supported Dex through the years when Dex needed to bend an ear, and when he wasn't physically nearby, Sage was never farther than a text or a phone call away.

"Nah. If it all fails, I'll come live with you." Dex had earned enough money off of the games he'd produced that he'd never have to worry about finances again, but he wasn't in the gaming business for the money. He'd been a gamer at heart since he was able to string coherent thoughts together, or at least it felt that way. "What's happening with the break you said you wanted to take? Are you going to Jack's cabin?" Their eldest brother Jack owned a cabin in the Colorado Mountains. Jack was an ex–Special Forces officer and a survival-training guide, and he and his fiancée Savannah spent most weekends at the cabin. Living and working in the concrete jungle didn't offer the type of escape Sage's brain had always needed.

"I've got another show or two on the horizon; then I'll take time off. But I think I want to do something useful with my time off. Find a way to, I don't know, help others instead of sitting around on my ass." He sipped his beer and tugged at the neck of his Baja hippie jacket. "How 'bout you? Any plans for vacay after the release?"

"Shit. You're kidding, right? My downtime is spent playing at my work. I love it. I'd go crazy sitting in some cabin with no connectivity to the real world."

"The right woman might change your mind." Sage took a swig of his beer.

"Dex date?" Regina tipped her glass to her lips. "Do you even know your brother? He might hook up once in a while, but this man protects his heart like it carries all of the industry secrets."

"Can we not go there tonight?" Dex snapped. He had a way of remembering certain moments of his life with impeccable clarity, some of which left scars so deep he could practically taste them every damn day of his life. He nurtured the hurt and relished in the joy of the scars, as his artistic and peace-seeking mother had taught him. But Dex was powerless against his deepest scar, and numbing his heart was the only way he could survive the memory of the woman he loved walking away from him four years earlier without so much as a goodbye.

"Whoa, bro. Just a suggestion," Sage said. "You can't replace what you never had."

Dex shot him a look.

Regina spun on her chair and then swung her arm over Dex's shoulder. "Incoming," she whispered.

Dex looked over his shoulder and met the stare of two hot blondes. His shoulders tensed and he sighed.

"It's not gonna kill you to make a play for one of them, Dex. Work off some of that stress." Sage glanced back at the women.

"No, thanks. They're all the same." Ever since the major magazines had carried the story about Dex's success, he'd been hounded by ditzy women who thought all he wanted to talk about was PC games.

Regina leaned in closer and whispered, "Not them. Fan boys, two o'clock."

Thank God.

"Hey, aren't you Dex Rem?" one of the boys asked.

Dex wondered if they were in college or if they had abandoned their family's dreams for them in lieu of a life of gaming. It was the crux of his concern about his career. He was getting rich while feeding society's desire to be couch potatoes.

"Remington, yeah, that's me," he said, wearing a smile like a costume, becoming the relaxed gamer his fans craved.

"Dude, *World of Thieves* is the most incredible game ever! Listen, you ever need any beta testers, we're your guys." The kid nodded as his stringy bangs bounced into his eyes. His friend's jaw hung open, struck dumb by meeting Dex, another of Dex's pet peeves. He was just a guy who worked hard at what he loved, and he believed anyone could accomplish the same level of success if they only put forth the effort. Damn, he hated how much that belief mirrored his father's teachings.

"Yeah?" Dex lifted his chin. "What college did you graduate from?"

The two guys exchanged a look, then a laugh. The one with the long bangs said, "Dude, it don't take a college degree to test games."

Dex's biceps flexed. There it was. The misconception that irked Dex more than the laziness of the kids who were just a few years younger than him. As a Cornell graduate, Dex believed in the value of education and the value of being a productive member of society. He needed to figure out the release date, not talk bullshit with kids who were probably too young to even be in a bar.

"Guys, give him a break, 'kay?" Regina said.

"Sure, yeah. Great to meet you," the longer-haired kid said.

Dex watched them turn away and sucked back his beer. His eyes caught on a woman at a booth in the corner of the bar. He studied the petite, brown-haired woman who was fiddling with her napkin while her leg bounced a mile a minute beneath the table. *Jesus.* Memories from four years earlier came rushing back to him with freight-train impact, hitting his heart dead center.

"I know how you are about college, but, Dex, they're kids. You gotta give them a little line to feed off of," Regina said.

Dex tried to push past the memories. He glanced up at the woman again, and his stomach twisted. He turned away, trying to focus on what Regina had said. *College. The kids. Give them a line to feed off of.* Regina was right. He should accept the hero worship with gratitude, but lately he'd been feeling like the very games that had made him successful were sucking kids into an antisocial, couch-potato lifestyle.

"Really, Dex. Imagine if you'd met your hero at that age." Sage ran his hand through his hair and shook his head.

"I'm no hero." Dex's eyes were trained on the woman across the bar. *Ellie Parker.* His mouth went dry.

"Dex?" Sage followed his gaze. "Holy shit."

There was a time when Ellie had been everything to him. She'd lived in a foster home around the corner from him when they were growing up, and she'd moved away just before graduating high school. Dex's mind catapulted back thirteen years, to his bedroom at his parents' house. "In the End" by Linkin Park was playing on the radio. Siena had a handful of girlfriends over, and she'd gotten the notion that playing Truth or Dare was a good idea. At thirteen, Dex had gone along with whatever his popular and beautiful sister had wanted him to.

She was the orchestrator of their social lives. He hadn't exactly been a cool teenager, with his nose constantly in a book or his hands on electronics. That had changed when testosterone filled his veins two years later, but at thirteen, even the idea of being close to a girl made him feel as though he might pass out. He'd retreated to his bedroom, and that had been the first night Ellie had appeared at his window.

"Hey, Dex." Regina followed his gaze to Ellie's table; her eyes moved over her fidgeting fingers and her bouncing leg. "Nervous Nelly?" she teased.

Dex rose to his feet. His stomach clenched.

"Dude, we're supposed to have a meeting. There's still more to talk about," Mitch said.

Sage's voice was serious. "Bro, you sure you wanna go there?"

With Sage's warning, Dex's pulse sped up. His mind jumped back again to the last time he'd seen her, four years earlier, when Ellie had called him out of the blue. She'd needed him. He'd thought the pieces of his life had finally fallen back into place. Ellie had come to New York, scared of what, he had no idea, and she'd stayed with him for two days and nights. Dex had fallen right back into the all-consuming, adoring, frustrating vortex that was Ellie Parker. "Yeah, I know. I gotta…" *See if that's really her.*

"Dex?" Regina grabbed his arm.

He placed his hand gently over her spindly fingers and unfurled them from his wrist. He read the confusion in her narrowed eyes. Regina didn't know about Ellie Parker. *No one knows about Ellie Parker. Except Sage. Sage knows.* He glanced over his shoulder at Sage, unable to wrap his mind around the right words.

"Holy hell," Sage said. "I've gotta take off in a sec anyway. Go, man. Text me when you can."

Dex nodded.

"What am I missing here?" Regina asked, looking between Sage and Dex.

Regina was protective of Dex in the same way that Siena always had been. They both worried he'd be taken advantage of. In the three years Dex had known Regina, he could count on one hand the number of times he'd approached a woman in front of her, rather than the other way around. It would take Dex two hands to count the number of times he'd been taken advantage of in the past few years, and Regina's eyes mirrored that reality. Regina didn't know it, but of all the women in the world, Ellie was probably the one he needed protection from the most.

He put his hand on her shoulder, feeling her sharp bones against his palm. There had been a time when Dex had wondered if Regina was a heavy drug user. Her lanky body reminded him of strung-out users, but Regina was skinny because she survived on beer, Twizzlers, and chocolate, with the occasional veggie burger thrown in for good measure.

"Yeah. I think I see an old friend. I'll catch up with you guys later." Dex lifted his gaze to Mitch. "Midnight?"

"Whatever, dude. Don't let me cock block you." Mitch laughed.

"She's an old...not a...never mind." *My onetime best friend?* As he crossed the floor, all the love he felt for her came rushing back. He stopped in the middle of the crowded floor and took a deep breath. *It's really you.* In the next breath, his body remembered the heartbreak of the last time he'd seen her. The time he'd never forget. When he'd woken up four years ago and found her gone—no note, no explanation, and no contact since. Just like she'd done once before when they were kids. The sharp, painful memory pierced his swollen heart. He'd tried so hard to forget her, he'd even moved out of the apartment to distance himself from the memories. He should turn away, return to his friends. Ellie would only hurt him again. He was rooted to the floor, his heart tugging him forward, his mind holding him back.

A couple rose from the booth where Ellie sat, drawing his attention. He hadn't even noticed them before. God, she looked beautiful. Her face had thinned. Her cheekbones were more pronounced, but her eyes hadn't changed one bit. When they were younger, she'd fooled almost everyone with a brave face— but never Dex. Dex had seen right through to her heart. Like right now. She stared down at something in her hands with her eyebrows pinched together and her full lips set in a way that brought back memories, hovering somewhere between worried and trying to convince herself everything would be okay.

Her leg bounced nervously, and he stifled the urge to tell her that no matter what was wrong, it would all be okay. Dex ignored the warnings going off in his mind and followed his heart as he crossed the floor toward Ellie.

To continue reading, buy
GAME OF LOVE (The Remingtons)

More Books By Melissa

BILLIONAIRES AFTER DARK SERIES

WILD BOYS AFTER DARK
Logan
Heath
Jackson
Cooper

BAD BOYS AFTER DARK
Mick
Dylan
Carson
Brett

LOVE IN BLOOM SERIES

SNOW SISTERS
Sisters in Love
Sisters in Bloom
Sisters in White

THE BRADENS at Weston
Lovers at Heart
Destined for Love
Friendship on Fire
Sea of Love
Bursting with Love
Hearts at Play

THE BRADENS at Trusty
Taken by Love
Fated for Love
Romancing My Love
Flirting with Love

BAYSIDE SUMMERS
Bayside Desires

The RYDERS
Seized by Love
Claimed by Love
Chased by Love
Rescued by Love
Thrill of Love

SEXY STANDALONE ROMANCE
Tru Blue
Wild Whiskey Nights

HARBORSIDE NIGHTS SERIES
Includes characters from the Love in Bloom series
Catching Cassidy
Discovering Delilah
Tempting Tristan
Chasing Charley
Breaking Brandon
Embracing Evan
Reaching Rusty
Loving Livi

More Books by Melissa
Chasing Amanda (mystery/suspense)
Come Back to Me (mystery/suspense)
Have No Shame (historical fiction/romance)
Love, Lies & Mystery (3-book bundle)
Megan's Way (literary fiction)
Traces of Kara (psychological thriller)
Where Petals Fall (suspense)

Acknowledgments

I'd like to thank my fans for begging, pleading, *demanding*, an edgier, racier version of The Bradens. Writing the After Dark series with the Wild and Bad brothers is so fun it borders on addicting, and I hope you enjoy them as much as I enjoy writing their love stories. As always, I hope you fall in love with each of the Wild and Bad brothers and their significant others. If you haven't read the Love in Bloom series yet, then dive in and read about the hot, sexy, and wickedly naughty characters in the Snow Sisters, The Bradens, The Remingtons, Seaside Summers, and The Ryders. You can also look forward to Harborside Nights, The Steeles, and The Stones.

If you don't yet follow me on Facebook, please do! We have such fun chatting about our lovable heroes and sassy heroines, and I always try to keep fans abreast of what's going on in our fictional boyfriends' worlds:
facebook.com/MelissaFosterAuthor

Remember to sign up for my newsletter to keep up-to-date with new releases and special promotions and events:
www.MelissaFoster.com/Newsletter

For a complete list of my available books, please visit:
www.melissafoster.com/melissas-books

I am indebted to my amazing team of editors and proofreaders, whose meticulous efforts help bring you the cleanest books possible. Thank you: Kristen Weber, Penina Lopez, Jenna Bagnini, Juliette Hill, Marlene Engel, and Lynn Mullan. Thank you, Elizabeth Mackey, for the gorgeous cover.

Love and gratitude to Les. As always, you are my true-life hero.

Melissa Foster is a *New York Times* and *USA Today* bestselling and award-winning author. Her books have been recommended by *USA Today's* book blog, *Hagerstown* magazine, *The Patriot*, and several other print venues. She is the founder of the World Literary Café, and Fostering Success. Melissa has painted and donated several murals to the Hospital for Sick Children in Washington, DC.

Visit Melissa on her website or chat with her on social media. Melissa enjoys discussing her books with book clubs and reader groups and welcomes an invitation to your event.

Melissa's books are available through most online retailers in paperback and digital formats.

www.MelissaFoster.com
www.MelissaFoster.com/Newsletter

CPSIA information can be obtained
at www.ICGtesting.com
Printed in the USA
LVHW021822121218
600214LV00005B/729/P

9 781941 480137